Change of Heart

For Mathew

Change of Heart

Shari Maurer

WestSide Books ®
Lodi, New Jersey

Published by WestSide Books
60 Industrial Road
Lodi, NJ 07644
973-458-0485
Fax: 973-458-5289

This is a work of fiction. All characters, places, and events
described are imaginary. Any resemblance to real people,
places, and events is entirely coincidental.

Library of Congress Cataloging-in-Publication Data

Maurer, Shari.
  Change of heart / by Shari Maurer. -- 1st ed.
    p. cm.
  Summary: When sixteen-year-old Emmi Miller learns she will die
without a heart transplant, she becomes aware of all she has been tak-
ing for granted, from her parents' love to her soccer ability, but gains
strength from new friend Abe.
  ISBN 978-1-934813-36-2
  [1. Sick--Fiction. 2. Medical care--Fiction. 3. Transplantation of or-
gans, tissues, etc.--Fiction. 4. Family life--New York--Fiction. 5.
High schools--Fiction. 6. Schools--Fiction. 7. Soccer--Fiction. 8.
New York (State)--Fiction.] I. Title.
  PZ7.M44554Ch 2010
  [Fic]--dc22
                                                        2010009039

International Standard Book Number: 978-1-934813-36-2
School ISBN: 978-1-934813-37-9
Cover design by David Lemanowicz
Interior design by David Lemanowicz

Printed in the United States of America
10 9 8 7 6 5 4 3 2 1

First Edition

Change of Heart

Prologue

If I had known "normal" could disappear so quickly, would I have appreciated it more? Would I have been less afraid to raise my hand in class? Would I have let my mother's complaints roll off my back?

Looking back to how it was before everything changed, I think I'd have done things differently. I'd have stopped to enjoy the smell of the cut grass on the soccer field—and been nicer to my brothers. I'd have eaten that hot fudge sundae, even when I felt kind of fat.

But it's easy to analyze this stuff when you have the perspective I do now.

I think when you're sixteen, you believe you're invincible. Or immortal. Maybe it's both?

When the most stressful thing in your life is winning a soccer game or what to wear to school, you take some really basic things for granted.

Like the love of your parents.

Or hanging with your friends.

Or the beating of your heart . . .

Part 1

1

"Don't give up!" I screamed to my teammates as I ran down the field.

Noelle and Lauren, two of my closest friends, took up the cry, chanting with me as we tried to get the ball away from the other team.

It was the Lower New York Division Soccer Championships, and my team was playing Nyack for the title and the right to go to Maryland to play in the East Coast Indoor Winter Tournament. That tournament was a chance to play against some of the best high school teams in the country, and more importantly, to be seen by college coaches scouting juniors and seniors for their teams. At this point in my life, my biggest dream—no, my only dream—was to play soccer in college. I had to get our team into that tournament!

The score was 0-0, with only a minute left in the game. It was one of those late fall days where the leaves stubbornly clung to the trees; there was the tiniest breeze, more balmy than chilly. Nyack's defender had the ball and her powerful kick shot it right to me. It bounced off my chest (let's hear it for small boobs!) and I got it to my feet. Then I started dribbling and the defender charged me. Faking around her, I was now a few steps from the goal. I kicked, and—SCORE!

I turned and shot two thumbs up to my best friend, Becca, who did a little dance in goal, her blond ponytail swinging back and forth as she moved.

"Thirty seconds left. Get back in position," Coach Daley yelled. She was right: we had to hold them another thirty seconds. We lined up and the other team tipped the ball. Their forward slipped and I scooped the ball with my foot, passing it to Noelle. She dribbled it a few feet and was attacked by Nyack's midfielder, a wide and imposing girl. But Noelle passed the ball back to me, and there were just twenty seconds left on the clock. I wove around two Nyack defenders and got near the goal again. Only ten seconds left. They told me later that everyone was on their feet cheering, but all I saw was the goalie and the net. I faked a kick to the right. She shifted to block, and I kicked hard to the left. SCORE!

Noelle and Lauren jumped on top of me, followed by the rest of the team. The smell of teenage-girl sweat overwhelmed me as I was crushed under the pile of my best buddies. Then Becca ran out of goal and pulled me out, giving me a huge hug. After the two teams lined up and we gave a "good game" slap of the hand to each of the Nyack players, I walked over to the sideline to pack my bag.

As I was pulling off my shin guards, I looked up to see Sam Hunter watching me from across the field. Yes, Sam

Hunter, as in "that totally hot baseball player in two of my classes who I didn't think knew I was alive." Sam waved to me and smiled; it was the kind of smile where his green-gold eyes crinkled and his whole face lit up.

Deep breath. How did I look? Omigod! I was unbelievably sweaty and my hair . . . well, my hair's awful even when I'm not playing soccer. I'd pulled it back into a ponytail, but, as always, a piece had managed to escape. I smoothed it back and waved at Sam, locking eyes with him for a second. He smiled again, mouthing, "Nice job."

I mouthed "Thanks" and smiled back at him, making sure to show my dimples. Becca always says she can tell how much I like a guy by how deep my dimples get when I smile at him.

One of Sam's buddies came over and they started talking, then they turned and walked away from the field.

"Did you just have a 'moment' with Sam Hunter?" Becca asked.

"I think so," I replied, still a little stunned by it.

"You won!" my little brother Eli yelled as he jumped on my back.

"Get off me," I said to him, standing up and looking across the field to see if Sam was still watching. He wasn't, and I turned my attention back to my brother. "Hey, Eli," I said, giving him a high five. Eli was nine and could never get enough high fives.

"That was great!" Eli said. Eli was a soccer player, like me. In fact, he was so good, he played on a team with eleven-year-olds. "Jem, did you see that second one?" Eli said to Jeremy, my other brother. "That goalie didn't know what hit her." Jeremy was twelve and more into baseball than soccer, but he humored us with feigned interest when he had to.

I watched across the field as Sam disappeared with his friend. He was almost six feet tall and built like a baseball player—broad shoulders, nicely shaped butt. I usually preferred soccer bodies; but in this case, I might have to make an exception.

Becca zipped her bag shut and I turned in her direction.

"Omigod! We're going to the Maryland tournament," I said, my attention shifting from the Sam Hunter miracle to the reality of our win.

At this point, my parents joined us. My mom took a sip of her ever-present coffee and smiled at me. I was never sure if it was genuine with her, or if she was just trying really hard to look as if she liked me. My dad gave me a big hug of congratulations. He gets it more than my mom does—he played soccer in college and is still active on an over-forty team.

"Look out, college scouts—we're coming at you!" Becca screamed, pounding her fist in the air. I whooped along with her.

"Careful, girls. You never know about these things," my mother said. I can always count on my mother to kill any buzz I might be feeling.

"Yeah, you're right, Mom," I replied, the words dripping sarcasm and anger. "There's no point thinking it might happen. In fact, maybe we shouldn't even bother going at all."

"That's not what I meant, Emmi," my mother said.

"April," my father said to her. Good, he was going to tell her she was being ridiculous. He should take my side— he's the one who got me into this soccer stuff in the first place and spent most of my games pacing the sidelines, shouting to me and videotaping. I think *he* wants me to get a scholarship and play in college even more than I do.

"I just don't want her to be disappointed if it doesn't work out," she said.

"Thanks for your support." I slammed my cleats and shin guards into my purple nylon bag, zipped the bag shut, and got up, stepping into my flip-flops on the way to our car.

"Emmi," my mother called. "I didn't mean it like that." But I wasn't listening to her. I heard someone behind me and said, "Go away." Except it wasn't my mother; it was Becca.

"Em, it's no big deal," my best friend said. It wasn't the first time Becca had to calm me down after I'd gotten into it with my mother.

"I *hate* her," I said. Becca started to say something but I cut her off. "Don't defend her."

"Wanna come over?" she asked. "I've got my car." Becca already had her driver's license, but my sixteenth birthday wasn't until next week. I was one of the youngest in my grade and never felt it as much as I did this year, when I watched all my friends get to drive before I did.

"C'mon," she said. "Let's plan that giant birthday bash

you've been begging me for." She knew I didn't want a birthday party at all, but I also didn't feel like going home, so I followed her to her car.

2

Off the soccer field, I didn't like being the center of attention. I usually sat quietly in most of my classes, too unsure of myself to answer any of the teacher's questions—even if I knew the answer. I've had a lot of teachers say that I didn't participate enough; in fact, they wouldn't let me take honors Spanish because I didn't talk enough in class.

The only place I've ever felt confident is the soccer field. And because I'm good, I play on both the school team and a travel team, along with Becca, Noelle, and Lauren. Last summer, Becca and I played on a team that got to go to Europe, where we played a lot of soccer (or *futbol*, as they call it there) and learned that European guys were way cooler than American ones. They didn't play games if they were interested; they just said "hi" and started talking to us. They even held the door open for us. I'd like to see the guys at my school do that. And for some reason, I wasn't shy at all over there.

But back home in New City, I was totally uncomfortable with Becca's challenge: to go up to Sam Hunter after class and invite him to the birthday party she insisted on giving me.

"I don't know why *you* can't invite him," I said when she announced the challenge.

"It's *got* to come from you," she said. And I didn't bother fighting her; I've known Becca since forever, and there is no way to change her mind once she has it set on something.

So Monday after the big win, I sat in Mr. Mistretta's eleventh-grade honors English class, absolutely unable to focus on a word the teacher said. I kept trying to make eye contact with Sam, hoping for another "moment" like the one we had at the field, but he was totally intent on Mr. Mistretta. After forty-five minutes of this, the bell finally rang. Everyone got up and headed toward the door, but I stalled, stacking and restacking my books, trying to walk out when Sam did; it worked and we ended up leaving at the same time.

"Hi," I said. *This is harder than I thought. What if he keeps walking and doesn't even acknowledge me? Or doesn't even remember talking to me on Saturday? Maybe it wasn't as big of a deal to him as it was to me.*

"Hi," he said. "Nice game Saturday. That second goal was amazing." He remembered!

"First goal wasn't too bad either," I said. *Omigod—what if he thinks I'm conceited?*

Sam smiled. Oooh, I really liked his smile. "Nope, the first one wasn't too bad either."

Enough chitchat. Time to ask the big question. "Um, I

was wondering. Um, my friend Becca's having a little birthday thing for me on Friday and, um, I just thought maybe, um, I don't know? Maybe you'd like to come?"

Was it an overly long pause, or did it just feel that way to me?

"Thanks, but I can't."

"Oh," I said and started walking away. *Can't, or doesn't want to? God, am I an idiot! Why did Becca push me into doing this?*

I left as quickly as I could, vowing never to get talked into something like that again. As I fled, I bumped right into Becca, who'd been hovering outside the class, waiting for the outcome.

"I can't believe you made me do that," I hissed at her. Sam walked past us and I kept my head down to avoid further humiliation.

"What'd he say?" she asked.

"He can't," I said, walking as quickly as I could toward my locker. It was time for this day to end, and I couldn't get out of there fast enough. Becca followed me.

" 'He can't' is not a definite rejection," she said. "Maybe he just can't." I pulled my books from my locker, trying to figure out which ones I needed to bring home. "Did you ask him why?"

"Why, so he could say he didn't want to right to my face? No. I didn't give him the chance."

"Maybe that's your problem—you never take a chance," Becca said. "Maybe he'd have told you that he has to baby-sit his little sister, or take his grandmother to bingo or something totally legit."

"You may be good at taking things head-on, but I'm happier getting my answer and leaving." I slammed my locker shut and started walking toward the buses. *I hate her sometimes. Why does she do this to me?* Becca continued following me. "Bec, maybe this whole birthday thing is a stupid idea. I don't need a big celebration; let's have the four of us at your house, like we usually do."

"You win," she said. "We'll keep it simple." She walked away and got on her bus.

I win? I've never won with Becca. Did I really win, or is something else up?

3

"Why am I wearing a blindfold?" I asked as we drove around in Becca's car that Friday night. Noelle was in the passenger seat, and Lauren was sitting in the back with me; it was pretty clear this wasn't going to be the simple birthday celebration Becca'd promised.

"It adds to the fun," Lauren told me. I couldn't see her, but I imagined her mischievous smile, the one usually reserved for boys she was about to make out with. Lauren wasn't pretty in the traditional sense: she had tiny brown eyes and a slightly crooked nose, but she made up for it with her incredible set of teeth and killer smile.

"I knew I couldn't have won," I mumbled to myself.

"A small celebration would *not* have fit the occasion," Becca said. "We weren't going to let you turn sixteen with just the four of us sitting around a cupcake at my house."

A minute later, the car stopped and we got out. I could hear the sounds of cars going by and people talking—parking lot sounds.

"Where are we?" I asked.

"Not telling," Lauren said, taking one of my hands while Becca took the other and they led me into a building. The crowd noises were louder now, and I smelled popcorn and disinfectant.

"Not the mall!" I hissed. "You know how much I hate the mall!" We didn't have some ordinary old mall in our town; no, we had the second-biggest mall in the state. And not only did it have 250 of your favorite mall stores, but it also had two food courts, a twenty-four-theater movie complex, an IMAX, an ice skating rink, a carousel, and a three-story Ferris wheel. It was humongous, concrete, ugly, always crowded, and my least favorite place to be. And I couldn't believe this was where they decided to take me for my sixteenth birthday. They were my best friends in the world—didn't they know anything about me?

"Do you trust us or not?" Lauren asked.

"Not. Is this one of your plots to meet guys?" No one answered me. I shook Lauren's hand away and tried to get the blindfold off. *Are people staring at me? What are they thinking?* Becca put my hands behind my back and continued guiding me along.

I could hear another door open and they led me up a few carpeted stairs. The unmistakable sound of pins being knocked down made me rip off my blindfold.

"Bowling?" I said. "*This* is the big plan? The last time I bowled was my eighth birthday party." I forgot to mention that the mall had a bowling alley, too.

This is my special sixteenth birthday celebration? Sure, it was an upscale bowling alley (is that an oxymoron?), but still. I didn't get it, but I figured if I was stuck here, I may as well try to enjoy it. They walked me over to the lanes, where a few of our guy soccer friends greeted us. We often ride the bus to away games together so we'd gotten pretty tight, but more brother-tight than boyfriend-tight. Actually, I did kiss Adam once (he's very cute—dark hair, dark eyes, and a perfect soccer body—have I mentioned how much I love soccer bodies?), but then he started dating this girl named Pam and that was that. Pam, the only non-soccer player in the group, was sitting next to him with her hands on his shoulder. Staking her territory, I guess.

I took a seat on one of the upholstered benches. At least it was a step up from the usual plastic bowling alley seats that are always sticky from spilled soda.

"Should we order something to eat?" Becca asked.

"Do they have anything here for us non-meat eaters?" I asked, the smell of fried food and overroasted hot dogs in the air. "Maybe some pizza or something?" I hadn't eaten meat since I was twelve; it was mostly in protest against cruelty to animals (even though I didn't mind killing and eating fish, which I knew made no sense).

"Stale bowling alley pizza? No way," Becca said. "They've got sushi, baby!"

I high-fived her. My favorite dinner! Maybe this was better thought out than I was giving them credit for. "Let's get the waiter."

"I'll find him," Lauren said.

"Do you think she'll come back?" I asked. Lauren was notorious for meeting guys and disappearing with them.

"She'll be back," Becca said, winking at Noelle. Noelle laughed and I knew something else was up. I looked at each of my friends, trying to figure out what they were pulling. The guys were focused on entering everyone's name into the bowling alley's computer.

"How 'bout girls versus guys?" Adam suggested.

"What d'you think, girls?" Becca asked us. "Can we take them?"

"No doubt about it," Noelle said and we all laughed.

"Can I take your order?" the waiter asked and I looked up.

It was Sam.

4

"Happy birthday," Becca whispered in my ear. "I think I see a big dimple smile coming on." She was absolutely right.

"Hey, Emmi," Sam said. He *couldn't* come; it wasn't that he didn't want to. "Happy birthday," he said, smiling at me. Our eyes met, and suddenly this was the best birthday ever.

"You work here?" *Duh.*

"Every Friday night," he said, pulling an order pad out of his apron. He was wearing one of those '50s retro bowling shirts in neon green, which happened to look great with his eyes.

"Oh," I said. There I was, out of conversation already!

"What would you like?" he asked.

"Becca said there's sushi. Was she making it up? I kind of smell, well, bowling alley food."

Sam laughed. "Yeah, we sell bowling alley food, but we also have salads and sushi, in case some girls come in."

"Do you get girls here?" I asked, going along with him.

"Once in a while. So there's no guarantee the sushi's fresh. Haven't been any girls in here for a few weeks."

"Yum. You make it sound so good. Maybe we should leave and go eat somewhere else," I said, pretending to start for the door.

"Don't go," he said. Again, our eyes met and locked.

"Maybe you can find me and the girls something fresh to eat," I said. *Where am I getting this nerve? It is so not like me.*

"What about the guys?" Sam asked.

"Give them some bowling alley food," I said and we laughed.

"Emmi, you're up," Brian called from the bowling lane. Adam was taking his turn on the "guys" lane, and everyone else was sitting on the benches.

"I haven't done this since I was eight," I told Sam.

"Good luck, then," he said. I walked away smiling and picked up a bowling ball, not sure if he was still watching me. I didn't want to turn around, so in case he was, I sauntered over to the line, swung back, and released the ball. It would've been a great story if I got a strike, but I'm not that lucky. At least it didn't go in the gutter, and it nipped a few pins so it wasn't total humiliation. My second ball fared slightly better, knocking down two more pins. I turned to see Sam still watching me; I shrugged my shoulders and he smiled. Then he pointed toward the kitchen, which I took to mean he was going to place our order.

"What's up with you and Hunter?" Brian asked me.

I've known Brian since kindergarten, when the soccer team was coed. We were the only two kids on the team who weren't picking blades of grass or fiddling with our shoelaces during the games.

"Don't know," I said, unable to suppress the huge smile on my face.

"Be careful," Brian said. "He's a player."

"What d'you mean?" I asked.

"C'mon, Emmi, you know the type," Brian said. "He's a big flirt, but he doesn't really date just one girl. He's more Lauren's type than yours." Then Becca bowled a strike and the whole group cheered. "Be careful," Brian warned.

"Suddenly you're my big brother," I snapped at him, getting up to take my turn. I grabbed the ball and flung it down the lane, where it landed in the gutter with a thud. I didn't know how to take this advice, but I also didn't want to be Sam's latest conquest.

Sam came back with our sodas too quickly for me even to think about what to do.

"Diet Coke with a lime," Sam said as he handed me my glass. I took it, but tried not to make eye contact with him. I couldn't deal with a player. If I was going to have a boyfriend (and it would've been really nice to have one) I wanted him to be a straight-up good guy, not someone just trying to get something. "You did say lime, right?" he asked. I nodded. "The hot dogs are ready. Should I bring them or do you want to wait for the sushi?"

"Guys, you want your food now, or do you want to wait for us?" I asked them.

"No hurry on the dogs; they've probably been ready since Wednesday," Sam said.

I didn't laugh or try to zing one back. The guys didn't answer—they were all too caught up in bowling. "Everything together's fine," I said, walking over to sit on the benches.

"What happened?" Becca asked as she sat down next to me.

"He's not as cute as I thought up close," I said. She looked at me with pure skepticism.

"Yeah, and the real answer is . . . ?" Becca asked.

"Isn't it your turn to bowl?" I asked. The bowling alley was suddenly becoming too noisy for me. "I need some air," I said. I picked up my coat and started toward the door.

"Where're you going?" Lauren asked. Noelle grabbed my hand and sat me down.

"Have you ever noticed when things get a little weird, you always try to run off?" Becca asked.

"Screw you," I answered.

"No, I'm serious," she said. "In the world of 'fight or flight,' you always pick flight."

"So now this is a therapy session?"

"Sorry, you're right. It's your birthday. All I'm saying is that once in a while you shouldn't run. You should stay and fight, or deal with it or whatever. But running away isn't always the solution to everything."

I looked at Sam across the room, then at my friends; I remembered it was my birthday and I was determined to have fun. Sam probably was just flirting; I shouldn't get so caught up in it. He was cute, though. But if he was a player, I didn't want to be some girl he was toying with. It happened to me last year with Matt Stenwick, and it was horrible. He was sweet as can be for about three weeks. Then when he tried to go too far at Lizzie King's party and I wouldn't let him, he told anyone who would listen what a tease I was.

I sighed.

"Who's up next?" I asked, trying to refocus on the game. "We have some butt to kick."

It turned out to be a fun night after all. And I smiled politely at Sam's attempted jokes, but when he saw I wasn't joking back, he didn't come back over as much. At one point I saw him looking over at me, but I quickly turned away. I didn't want to get hurt, and I didn't need the distraction. There were only two weeks left until the Maryland tournament, and I had a lot of schoolwork to do on top of it. I kept repeating that in my head, trying not to look over at Sam as he waited on the other tables.

5

Training and studying took up most of my waking hours over the next two weeks, and there was no time to think about Sam. Coach Daley had kicked things up a bit and now we were practicing three hours every afternoon. By the time I got home, I could barely move; I'd take a shower, have a quick dinner, and go up to my room to do homework. Being in several honors classes gave me a big chunk of homework each night; between that and all the soccer practice, I was getting run-down and felt a cold coming on. I was trying not to let the sneezing and coughing distract me as I picked up the first book to start studying.

I usually started with math, finding it easier to get the math problems out of the way before I started on the reading for English and history. After I got done with math and English, I rewarded myself by signing on to Facebook. Becca was online.

Emmi: *Hey, Bec. What's up?*

Becca: *Mom's working. House is quiet. U?*

Emmi: *Studying. Math and English down, 3 more 2 go. I'm tired.*

| **Becca:** | *Me 2. 3 days till the big tournament. I'm totally psyched. I think we're going to win it.* |
| **Emmi:** | *U think big. I think ur crazy, but I like it.* |

A new chat popped up on my screen. It was Sam!

| **Sam:** | *Hey.* |

Oh. My. God. We'd smiled at each other a time or two since the bowling alley, but I had tried to keep him at a distance. I quickly wrote to Becca.

| **Emmi:** | *Bec. OMG. Sam Hunter just chatted me. g2g.* |

I turned my attention back to Sam.

| **Emmi:** | *What's up?* |
| **Sam:** | *Have u done the math hw yet?* |

Oh. He needs homework help.

Emmi:	*Yeah. Wasn't too bad.*
Sam:	*What did u get for #3?*
Emmi:	*Is that y ur writing – for homework help?*
Sam:	*And to say hello* ☺

Yeah, right.

| **Emmi:** | *Don't they have extra help for u dumb jocks?* |
| **Sam:** | *Yeah, haven't I seen u there sometimes?* |

Was he flirting? It was so hard to know when everything's in writing and you can't see someone's face.

| **Emmi:** | *Careful. I wouldn't insult me and ask for homework help at the same time.* |
| **Sam:** | *Point taken. I think ur gr8. So what did you get for #3?* |

Emmi:	*Ur persistent.*
Sam:	*Yep. That's something u should know about me.*

Was he trying to tell me something? Or was he playing me like Brian said he would? Maybe he was the real deal and I should give him a chance.

Sam:	*So what's the answer 2 #3?*
Sam:	*Just kidding. I was actually trying to find an excuse to chat.*

Really?! Now what do I say? I sneezed and went across the room to get a tissue. This also bought me time to think.

Sam:	*u there?*
Emmi:	*I'm here. The answer to #3 is 42.6.*
Sam:	*I got that, too. Maybe I'm not such a dumb jock.*
Emmi:	*Prove it. What did u get for #8?*
Sam:	*-17.4*

Pretty impressive. That'd been a hard one.

Emmi:	*Okay, I have officially removed the "dumb jock" label from your profile.*
Sam:	*Thanks. I was worried.*
Sam:	*So what r u doing this weekend?*

Oh my God, was he asking me out?

Emmi:	*Y? Do you need help with your homework?*
Sam:	*Ha. No, I thought maybe you'd like to do something.*

Oh my God, he was asking me out! But I was going to Maryland this weekend. Why did the most exciting weekend of my sports life have to coincide with getting asked out by this amazing guy that I would have thought was absolutely beyond me? Life was not fair.

Emmi: *I would love to, but we're going to Maryland for a soccer tournament.*
Sam: *Another time, then.*
Emmi: *Yeah, another time would be great.*
Sam: *c u 2morrow.*
Emmi: *ttyl*

I signed off, and for the first time in my life, I hated soccer. I mean, how could it come between me and a date with a totally hot guy? Okay, a hot guy who could be a player, but one I might like to give a chance. *Will he ever ask me out again, or did I blow it? If he asked me once, he'll ask me another time, won't he?*

I sneezed again and brought the entire box of tissues over to the computer. My nose was red and running and I was exhausted, but my excitement about something possibly happening with Sam gave me new energy to complete the rest of my homework.

6

The next day I was pretty nervous to see Sam at school, and when I walked into math class, he was already in his seat. I wasn't sure if I should go over and say hi, but as I was deciding, he looked up at me and gave me a huge smile. I decided to play it cool; I smiled back and took my seat. Every once in a while I caught him looking at me; it was becoming very difficult to focus on math . . . and on English a few periods later. What a relief that he only had two classes with me.

Somehow I made it through the next few days. I was enjoying flirting with Sam, and I fell back in love with soccer, but my cold was getting worse. I tried everything I could think of to make it go away: I flooded myself with orange juice hoping the Vitamin C would help; I took zinc tablets I found in my mother's medicine cabinet, which claimed to shorten the length of a cold. But nothing worked. By Friday, on the bus heading for Maryland, I felt like crap. My nose wouldn't stop running, and I coughed so much I couldn't manage a full sentence.

My mother worried about me going to the tournament sick, but I tried not to sneeze or cough too much in front of her so she wouldn't know how bad it was. I was glad this was a tournament where only Coach Daley and her assistant were there to chaperone and that the parents weren't with us. My mother never would have let me play if she'd seen how bad I looked. I took some antihistamine, which stopped the runny nose, but it didn't help the cough much.

"Emmi, you sound awful," Coach Daley said as we got off the bus at the stadium. "I heard you coughing the whole way down."

"I'm fine," I told her. I'd worked too long and hard to let anything stop me from playing in this tournament.

"Everyone, grab only your soccer stuff," the coach instructed us as we left the bus. "We'll go to the hotel after the first game and you can get your luggage then."

Becca tossed me my purple nylon soccer bag and we walked into the stadium.

"Do you think we'll know who the scouts are?" Becca asked me.

"They'll be the ones with the college logos on their shirts," I said.

"Do you think it'll be that obvious, or will they not want us to know who they are? Like a spy kind of thing?" Becca winked at me and I punched her arm affectionately, the excitement of the event pushing me along despite how crappy I felt.

Becca and I met when we were nine and were both picked for our town's travel soccer team. I wasn't sure I wanted to play, but because my father had played in college, he was really into it. Even though I was good enough to make the team, I didn't have much confidence. But Becca was my complete opposite: she marched right in, like it was her right. She also decided to make me her project, inviting me over on non-practice days and showing me her favorite moves as we'd kick the ball around. After keeping this up for a while, we both got pretty good. We were always pushing each other, challenging each other to do better. It was good to have a friend like that.

"You know, if we don't get a scholarship for college, we could always go back to Europe and play," I said.

"I like that idea! *Viva la Europe!*" she said, raising her fist in the air and laughing. As we walked, I felt like I was breathing better. I thought maybe I just needed fresh air and it was the stale air on the bus that made me cough so much.

After we'd all gotten into our uniforms, we sat on the field in a circle doing stretches. Astroturf is much pricklier than grass and it was uncomfortable, but it felt good to stretch out after the long, cramped bus ride. I started coughing again and Becca shot me a look.

We won the first game, then two more the next day, qualifying us for the finals on Sunday. I scored a few goals each game, but it wasn't as easy for me as it usually was; I was winded and really had to push myself. A few times I missed opportunities to score—shots I never would have missed otherwise. And I'd really wanted to show off for the scouts, but Becca and I decided they were either not there

33

at all, or else very good at blending in with the crowd. Or, maybe they were waiting for the finals to see the cream of the crop.

I woke up Sunday morning feeling achy, with my cough becoming more frequent and heavy with phlegm.

"Em, I don't think you should play," Becca said as we got ready in our room.

"You're just saying that so the scouts don't see me," I shot at her.

"Don't be ridiculous. Look at you—you're half dead."

I turned to the mirror and saw a very pale version of myself. I tried to ignore the chills, knowing they were the sign of fever—and that I was really sick. "I'll just take Advil and I'll be fine," I said, going into my bag to find the bottle. I really wasn't sure I was going to be fine, but I had no choice—I was playing in that game no matter what. And just to make it convincing to anyone who looked at me that I was okay, I put on some blush. *There, I look much better now*, I told myself.

We went down to the hotel restaurant and found Lauren sitting at a table, looking at a menu.

"You saved us a seat," Becca said, sliding into one of the empty chairs. I took the other one, and Lauren didn't say a word; she was staring at me.

"What?" I asked, opening the menu. But nothing I saw appealed to me; I was nauseous from all of the stuff dripping down my throat. Yet I knew I couldn't play without eating something first.

"Go ahead," Becca said to Lauren, "tell her how bad she looks."

"Leave me alone," I said to Becca as Noelle walked into the restaurant and pulled up a chair to join us.

"You look like crap," Noelle said, looking at me.

"Your blush is uneven," Lauren said, reaching over to rub my cheek to fix it. "Wow, you're burning up, Emmi!"

"Leave me alone, okay?" I said and started to get up. But I was a little wobbly so I sat back down. Forget "fight or flight." I just needed food. "Where's the waitress?" I asked. I was sweating and wanted ice water one minute, then needed hot tea for my chills the next.

"She said she'd be over in a sec," Noelle said. "But I'm going to tell Coach what's going on."

Coach Daley was a great soccer coach, but she wasn't particularly nurturing or maternal. She'd been a star player in high school and still had a little of that swagger, even if she was slightly overweight now. She sat eating alone, reading; her frizzy reddish hair peeked out from her white Nike cap, which bobbed up and down as she chewed. I'd never seen her at a game without that stupid hat.

"Please don't," I begged. "I'm going to be okay. There's only one more game, and you know there isn't anybody on the bench who's as good as I am." They stared at me, knowing it was true. "Once we win the game, I'll climb on that bus and go to sleep for the whole trip home—and I can rest until we start playing in the spring."

"That's a stupid idea," Noelle said. Of the four of us, Noelle was the biggest worrier—and the most practical.

"You have to promise to take yourself out of the game if you get any worse," Becca said, uncertainty clouding her eyes.

I met her gaze and promised. But if any of them had even a hint of what would happen at that game, or about what was going on as I played, they'd have tied me to that chair and dragged the coach over to hear the whole story. But they didn't know—none of us did—so instead they all just nodded and went along with me.

7

By the time the bus pulled into the stadium parking lot after breakfast, I was feeling a little better. The drip in the back of my throat was still there, but I wasn't as achy. Feeling the way I did on that cold, gray winter day, I'd have been happy to stay under the covers reading a book or watching TV instead of playing another game. To add to my misery, we stepped off the bus into a gust of wind that made me shiver; I walked as quickly as I could to the stadium entrance, not waiting for my friends to catch up to me.

Inside the locker room, we sat on the metal benches beside the lockers. Becca sat next to me.

"You okay?" she whispered to me.

"I'm good."

"Do you think when we were little, we'd ever have imagined being in a game like this?" Becca asked. I squeezed Becca's hand and listened to Coach Daley's pep talk.

Then we ran out of the locker room and onto the field.

Dribbling the soccer ball between my feet, everything seemed normal. I passed the ball back and forth with Noelle as we ran down the field.

Soon the ref blew her whistle and called "Time!" We got into our positions and I felt good. I felt hyped; I felt invincible. And then I sneezed. Okay, maybe not invincible.

I was not 100 percent during this game. I'm not sure I was even 50 percent, but I pushed myself as hard as I could. By the second half, we were behind 1-0. Becca had allowed a rare goal and I was starting to get nervous. I was also starting to feel very tired. Usually, I could play a sixty-minute game and still have energy left to run back to the locker room in a full sprint. But that day I was having trouble running, and I got winded with every play.

But I had to get over this weakness I was feeling; we had a timeout and I drank some Gatorade. Then Coach Daley walked over to me.

"Emmi, I'm taking you out," she said.

"Why? I'm fine."

"I don't think you are," she said.

I took another sip of Gatorade. "I'm rejuvenated now. Really. It's only three more minutes. I can do it." Coach looked at me and I could see how torn she was. But I didn't care; I *had* to finish this game. "Besides, I figured out what we have to do. Noelle, I have a plan—come here."

Noelle walked over and I explained how we were going to bring the ball down the field and get past the opponent.

"You're one of the most strategic players I've ever coached," Coach Daley said.

"Which means you'll let me play, right?" I asked. She shifted from one foot to the other. "I'll be fine," I promised.

"If I see any sign that you're not okay, I'm pulling you out." I was running back on the field before she could finish her sentence, so I turned and gave her a thumbs-up.

Lauren in-bounded the ball to Noelle; the other team almost stole it, but Noelle was able to pass it out to me. I started running down the field toward the goal; the other team's defender charged me and I tipped it back to Noelle. Next I ducked past the defender, and Noelle passed the ball back to me. Now there were only a few feet between me and the goal. I ran as hard as I could, but I could feel my chest burning. My legs began shaking as I took a few more steps and then . . . everything was black.

8

I woke up in the middle of the field and had no idea what had happened. I tried to get up and keep running, but I couldn't even stand.

"Damn it, Emmi," I heard Coach yell as she ran over to me. Becca had already come down from the goal and was standing next to me. "I told you you shouldn't be playing!" Coach shouted.

"I've got to get back up," I said, but I could barely talk. "I've got to finish."

"Emmi, stop it," Becca said. "It's not that important." I looked at her like she had two heads. Winning was *never* not important.

A man came over and introduced himself as the tournament doctor. He got me to my feet and guided me to the side of the field, with Becca walking beside me every step. The other girls were trying to crowd me, but Coach shooed them away. I saw two girls on the other team look at each other with "We win!" smiles and I started to cry.

"I'm fine," I said. "Put me back in."

"Will you shut up with the 'I'm fine' stuff, already," Becca said.

"They think it's over, but it's not," I said through my tears. "We can still win." The doctor sat me down on the bench.

"I'm going to take your blood pressure," he said, taking out a blood pressure cuff and wrapping it around my arm.

I tried to watch the rest of the game while he took my pulse and my temperature, then listened to my heart and shone a light in my eyes. With me sidelined, we never got the goal we needed to tie up the game. We lost, 1-0.

The doctor declared me well enough to participate in the trophy ceremony, so I was able to join my team when we received our second-place awards. I still felt a little dizzy, but the burning in my chest was gone. Coach Daley didn't leave my side, meanwhile, and she insisted I call my parents to tell them what happened. When I made the call, I had to hold my cell away from my ear—my mother was screaming so loud. I tried to quell her panic, reminding her I was calling her myself, so it wasn't that bad. But she still insisted I let her talk to the tournament doctor herself. He told her exactly what he told me: that I was probably dehydrated and should drink and rest.

As we left the stadium, everyone on the bus was pretty bummed, making it much quieter than it had been on the way down. We stopped at a sandwich place to buy lunch for the ride home, where I bought a mozzarella cheese and tomato sandwich, but I didn't touch it. I was still lethargic—a combination of achy exhaustion and disappointment over the loss—and I ended up sleeping for the whole trip back. When we got to the school parking lot, we got off the bus and Becca drove me back to my house. My chest hurt from all the coughing I'd done, and all I wanted was to climb into bed. But I had to make a show of saying hello to my parents and my brothers.

Eli grabbed my trophy and Jeremy tried to wrestle him for it. I didn't even care.

"I'm going upstairs to lie down for a while," I announced to my parents. All I wanted was to curl up in my bed and go back to sleep.

"Are you sure you're okay?" my mother asked, reaching to feel my forehead.

"Yeah," I said. "I'll be better in the morning."

"I'll wake you up for dinner."

"That's okay—I'm not really hungry. If I want something later, I'll grab it then."

As soon as I got to my room, I put my head on the pillow and fell into a deep sleep.

9

I have one of the greatest beds ever. It's a double with a pillow top, which is exactly like it sounds, a pillow sewn to the top of your bed. You climb in and sink into this cloud of comfort. And my pillow's awesome, too—it's made out of this spongy foam that molds to the shape of your head, cocooning it in incredible softness. With my down comforter on top of it all, it's hard to get out of bed in the morning.

But the day after I got back from Maryland, it was almost impossible to get up. I could barely lift my head, and my nose was totally stuffed—I couldn't breathe out of it at all. I pulled myself up and tried to lean against my headboard; my soccer jersey and sweats, which I'd slept in the whole night, were sticking to me. Feeling pretty bad by now, I was hot one minute and then shivering the next. I couldn't remember ever being this sick.

"Good morning," Mom said, poking her head into my room. She was way too cheery for this early in the morning; it was probably the coffee. She always had her first cup as soon as she woke up, thanks to a coffeemaker with auto timer. And she didn't even switch to decaf later on; it was a constant infusion of caffeine. It sure explained a lot about my mother.

"Hi," I managed to say. My throat was hoarse and it tickled to talk. Mom walked over to my bed and felt my forehead.

"Still pretty warm," she said. "You're staying home today." I sank back into my pillow and closed my eyes.

"I knew going to that tournament was crazy," she said.

"Please, Mom," I rasped. "Don't start."

My mom took a deep breath and sat next to me on the bed.

"I'm sorry I can't stay home this morning," she said as she stroked my hair. "I have a meeting with the superintendent, but I'll leave early. Will you be okay until then?"

I nodded. It hurt to speak. My mom was an accountant for our school district, and I knew she needed to be there, but I didn't mind being alone. I just wanted to rest.

"Let me bring you some Advil," Mom said. "Are you hungry?"

I shook my head no.

"There's some soup in the fridge you could reheat," she said. "Or let me make you some instant oatmeal."

"I'm fine," I said, thinking about how many times I had said that in yesterday's game and it turned out I wasn't.

"Here's some water," she said. "Please try to drink some of it. When I spoke to the tournament doctor yesterday, he said he thought you might be dehydrated. We're out of Gatorade, but I'll get some on the way home. Anything else you need?" I shrugged. Right now I didn't want anything but to go back to sleep.

She kissed me on the forehead. I heard "Love you" as I drifted off.

10

Two more days went by without me getting out of bed. After the third day my mom brought me to the doctor, where I was subjected to a throat swab (strep?), blood tests (Lyme disease or mono?), and a very thorough physical (all of the above or something else?). Everything came back negative or normal, so the doctor thought it was probably a virus and I would just have to wait it out.

My mother encouraged me to drink fluids as much as possible, so basically I drank, slept, and peed all day. The true measure of how sick I was? I had absolutely no interest in turning on my computer or answering my cell phone. Not even to see if Sam wanted to do some online flirting. Becca brought my work home from school and it was piling up in the corner near my bedroom door.

One afternoon I decided to brave a trip to the first floor of my house. Jeremy and Eli were playing video games in the family room and I could hear my mother making dinner in the kitchen. I took the stairs one at a time, gripping the railing for support. The old stairs creaked after every step, making my head start to ache. My legs were a little wobbly and my heart pounded. I was on the third-to-last step when suddenly I was lying on the floor at the bottom of the staircase. My brothers were on both sides of me and my mother came running in from the kitchen.

"What happened?" Mom screamed.

"I don't know," Eli said. "We heard a thud and found Emmi at the bottom of the stairs."

I looked at them and tried to find my voice. "I was almost at the bottom and then—I guess I slipped."

"Can you move?" Jeremy asked. I wiggled my toes and fingers and bent my legs and arms.

"I think so."

"Let's get her to the couch," Mom said. Jeremy took one arm and Mom the other and they lifted me to my feet. "You need to eat," Mom said and guided me to the kitchen table. She put some vegetable broth and noodles in a bowl and nuked it. The soup tasted pretty good. Maybe she was right—maybe I just needed to eat.

Afterward, I didn't feel like going back upstairs so I turned on the TV and crashed on the family room couch. It was chocolate brown Ultrasuede and sturdy enough to stand my wrestling brothers who often ate on the couch even when they weren't supposed to. Like my bed, it was very soft and comfortable. Mom said she sat on every couch in the county to find it and I was grateful as I wrapped my blanket around me, put my head on the pillow, and watched some mindless television program. I must have fallen asleep because when I woke up it was dark outside and I could hear my parents talking in the kitchen.

"The doctor said it's a virus," my mother was saying. "She just needs a little more rest."

"April, you said she passed out again," my father said. "I think we need to push a little more and get some answers." I heard my mother step away from the table and go to the counter to pour a cup of coffee.

"Larry's wife is a pediatric oncologist at Children's Hospital in the city. Why don't we ask her advice?" my dad suggested.

"She doesn't have cancer," my mother snapped. Cancer? How did I go from having a virus to having cancer?

"No, I don't think she has cancer, but I do think we could use another opinion. Let's see if she can recommend an expert for a consultation." Did they really think I could have cancer?

"Mom," I called weakly from the couch. My parents both came into the room. "Why do you think I have cancer?"

"No one said you have cancer," my father said. "If you overheard us, it was just that Larry's wife is an oncologist at a good hospital in the city and I think you should see someone there if you keep passing out."

"I don't *keep* passing out," I corrected him. "I only did it once."

"Which one are you counting, the time on the soccer field or today on the stairs?" he asked.

"Okay, twice." My mom sat down on the couch next to me and took my hand.

"Her fever's down," Mom said. "Maybe she's on the upswing."

"I'm going to make an appointment with someone at Children's Hospital for next Monday," my father said. "If she's better by then, we'll cancel it."

We all agreed, but I had a feeling I wasn't going to be better by then, because my heart had started to beat funny—like a sudden, racing BOOM, BOOM, BOOM—that went on for a few minutes and then stopped. I hadn't told my parents about it and knew I should, but I kept thinking it'd stop. It probably didn't mean anything—maybe I was just nervous or it could be a side effect of the cold medicines I was taking. I came up with all kinds of possible explanations but the more I thought about it, the more I worried. BOOM, BOOM, BOOM is not normal. Something really *was* wrong.

11

Monday came and with no improvement in sight, Mom packed me off toward New York City and the "experts" at Children's Hospital. I still hadn't told anyone about my heart pounding; it'd only happened a few more times and I convinced myself it was going away. But most viruses didn't knock you out for weeks, make you pass out, or cause a BOOM, BOOM, BOOM in your chest. What was wrong with me?

My mom was chattering away beside me but I wasn't listening. I don't think she expected an answer; she was nervous and didn't know what else to do. She was going on about the pediatrician Larry's wife had recommended: she had a column in a prestigious parenting magazine and often appeared on television when they needed an expert pediatrician to comment on a news story. She was affiliated with Children's Hospital but had private offices in a posh apartment building on Park Avenue. As a favor to Larry's wife, she'd squeezed us into her busy schedule.

The waiting room was divided into a sick waiting area and a well one, all designed to keep kids occupied and entertained while they waited; each side had toys for little kids and computers for older ones, and next to the computers were antibacterial wipes and reminders to wipe them down after each use. I crumpled into my chair in the sick waiting area, grateful for the chance to rest—the short walk from the parking garage had tired me out. As I watched the sick kids play, I wondered how sick they could be if they still had enough energy for it.

Soon we were ushered into an exam room and I was given a soft and comfortable lavender terry cloth robe to change into, unlike at my local pediatrician's office where they gave us paper robes that ripped if you pulled the tie too tight. Other than feeling so crappy, I was starting to enjoy this Park Avenue thing.

After her nurse asked some preliminary questions, Dr. Preston sauntered into the exam room in her three-inch heels and designer suit. She turned to my mother and said, "So, Mommy, what's wrong today?" *Mommy? I'm not three years old.* How about "Mrs. Miller" or something that sounded less obnoxious? My mother didn't seem to notice or be bothered by it, and she proceeded to describe what had happened to me in the past two weeks, highlighting the fainting episodes and making them sound dramatic. The two of them bantered back and forth, discussing me as if I weren't even there. It was like watching some strange medical talk show starring my mother and Dr. Preston. Worn out, I lay back on the exam table and closed my eyes; this would be a great time to take a nap until they were ready for me.

"Okay, Emmi," I heard Dr. Preston say in a sing-song

voice. "Are we ready for our exam?" I opened my eyes and sat up. Was this chick for real? "Let's pull our robe open and let me have a listen."

I rolled my eyes skeptically at my mother; she just shrugged and looked over at Dr. Preston with an enamored smile. Dr. Preston put the stethoscope to my chest with an elaborate motion she probably invented to distract toddlers and listened for a minute.

I watched as her bright phony smile turned into a frown of genuine concern.

12

"What is it you're hearing?" Mom asked, the panic clear in her voice.

"Shh," Dr. Preston said to her. "Emmi, breathe in."

I did as I was told.

"Is something wrong?" my mother prodded. Didn't she hear the part where Dr. Preston told her to stop talking?

"I don't know," Dr. Preston said. When she removed the stethoscope, the look on her face made me wonder if she'd ever uttered those words before.

"Sometimes my heart goes BOOM, BOOM, BOOM," I said quietly.

My mother bolted out of her chair. "Why didn't you tell me that?" she demanded.

"I thought it'd go away," I said. *Don't yell at me, Mom. I'm scared enough already.*

Dr. Preston was still studying me; then she took out her blood pressure cuff and put it around my arm. Now things were serious and she was very, very quiet.

"Doctor, what are you thinking?" my mother asked.

"I'm thinking she should see a cardiologist for further

tests," she replied, taking my pulse. She proceeded to feel my neck and take my pulse there, on both sides. Next she asked me to lie down and continued to examine me. When she was done, she said, "I'm going to call a friend of mine to see if she can see Emmi today."

Today? This was no joke. I closed my eyes and tried not to let my mother or Dr. Preston see my tears.

There are times I hate my mother, and then there are other times when she comes through for me; this was one of those times. Probably realizing that her rising panic wasn't helping me, she calmed down, walked over to the exam table, handed me a tissue, and bent down to kiss my cheek. "Don't worry, honey. We're going to figure this out." She was so strong but I was crumbling.

Mom called Dad on the way uptown to Children's Hospital. Dad left work right away to be with us—setting off even more alarm bells about how serious this was. Dad's a lawyer in the city and has these really high-powered clients; he's always working long hours and I didn't ever remember a time when he left work in the middle of the day except for major emergencies. Now my mind raced from one horrible possibility to another; I wanted to ask my mother what she thought it might be, but I was too afraid of the answer.

I liked Dr. Leavens, the cardiologist, right away. She was tiny even in her heels, and she had the most gorgeous auburn hair. She treated me like an adult and spoke directly to me. I told her about passing out and my heart pounding; she listened and asked questions about whether I'd gained weight and what sort of activities made me tired. I told her that everything I did wore me out. My parents held hands as Dr. Leavens and I spoke; it'd been a long time since I had seen them do that, so I knew they were very worried.

Next Dr. Leavens put this clamplike thing on the end of my finger that glowed red and told them how much oxygen was in my blood.

"87—not as high as I'd like," she said. "This is making me concerned; let's see what the other tests show." I didn't like what she was saying, but at least she was telling it straight. I spent the day learning new words like "echo" and "EKG," which stood for "echocardiogram" and "electrocardiogram." The EKG was pretty simple; they put stickers on my chest and hooked wires to the stickers. Then they told me to lie still for a second and it was over. The echo was easy too, but the technician squirted a clear gel on my chest and then rolled a wand over my chest and poked it under my ribs and near my throat. As she worked, a computer monitor beside us showed pictures of my heart with colorful blobs of color that I couldn't read.

After all the tests were over, Dr. Leavens sent me home with several prescriptions, along with orders to rest and lower my salt intake. I took deep breaths as we left the office and tried not to panic too much as I heard phrases like "viral myocarditis" and "heart failure."

Once we got home, I Googled "viral myocarditis" to see if I would be okay; but then I clicked off the site before I could get the answer—I wasn't sure I really wanted to know.

13

Several weeks and doctors' appointments later, I still didn't feel better. Dr. Leavens tried different medicines but nothing got me back to normal, the way I was before I got sick. Despite all the rest and pills, I was constantly tired and wiped out by the smallest effort. There was no way I could get through a school day so a tutor came to my house in the mornings. My teachers e-mailed my assignments, and now, teachers who barely knew me because I was so quiet in class were suddenly e-mailing me several times a day. I wasn't up for a lot of phone calls so my friends e-mailed and we texted and talked on Facebook when I felt up to it. By now, my computer and cell had become my lifelines that kept me connected to what used to be my real life.

I logged on one evening and saw Sam was online. I hadn't had any contact with him since I'd gotten sick, and I'd chalked it up to "out of sight, out of mind." Staring at his screen name, the shy side of me debated the curious side of me about Facebook-chatting him.

Sam: *R u there?*

Decision made for me! What do I say?

Emmi: *Yep.*

That's a grabber.

Sam: *Where have u been? Haven't seen u in a month.*

Sam: *The rumors are flying.*

Emmi: *What are they saying?*

People are talking about me? That's weird.

Sam: *Let's see: Rehab? Hiding a pregnancy? Cancer?*

Emmi: *Ouch. Awful—and totally wrong.*

Sam: *So what's going on?*

Emmi: *I had a virus. It went to my heart and now I'm in heart failure. They're giving me meds, but they're not helping enough. I go back 2 the hospital 2morrow for more tests. I'm 2 tired for school, so I have a tutor at home.*

Oh God, was that too much information?

Sam: *I had $10 on rehab, so I guess I'm out some $$.*

Emmi: *Not funny.*

Sam: *Sorry.*

Sam: *Not sure what I should say.*

Emmi: *It's OK. I'm not sure what to say either. I probably shouldn't have told you all of that.*

Sam: *No, I'm glad you did.*

Sam: *What can I do 4 u?*

Wow, he was the first person besides Becca to ask that.

Emmi: *idk. Chatting is nice.*

Sam: *Consider it done. I'll be your chat buddy.*
       Talk 2 u 2morrow, chat buddy. Feel good.

Emmi: *ttyl*

Emmi: *Sam?*

Sam: *What?*

Emmi: *Thanks.*

I logged off, ecstatic. Sam talked to me! He wanted to be my chat buddy! "Chat buddy"—it sounded so cute. I pushed my chair away from my desk and ran downstairs. By the time I reached the bottom of the staircase I was winded. I sat down on the bottom step and tried to catch my breath. My father saw me and sat down next to me on the step.

"You okay, honey?" he asked.

But I couldn't answer him. My heart was pounding and I tried to take a deep breath but couldn't. It was like a big, fat elephant was sitting on my chest and I couldn't breathe. My arms were shaking and I tried to stand up, but I was trembling too much for my legs to support me. Why couldn't I breathe? What was happening to me?

My dad saw the panic in my eyes. "I'm going to call the doctor," he said and headed for the phone. He came back and sat next to me, leaving a message with Dr. Leavens's service. "I wonder how long it'll take her to call back," he said. We sat on the step and Dad put his arm around me. I tried to steady my breathing and leaned into my dad, nestling there. *What's taking her so long to call back? What if they can't find her? What if she doesn't call back?*

When the phone finally rang, Dr. Leavens said to come to the emergency room at Children's Hospital.

"She thinks you'll be okay for the forty-minute ride," he said. "Your mother's at the mall with the boys. I'll call her on the way in and tell her what's going on." He brought me my coat, pulled me up off the step, and helped me put on the coat. I felt like a baby as he guided my arms into the sleeves and I looked up at him with a grateful expression. Then he put his arm around me and walked me slowly out to his car.

14

They admitted me to the hospital. Even though I was feeling better, Dr. Leavens was concerned about my shortness of breath and wanted to observe me for a few days. If I'd known this was a possibility, I'd have packed some pajamas and brought my pillow; instead, I was stuck in one of those awful hospital gowns and had to use their hard, lumpy hospital pillow. Sleeping would have been nice, but it was impossible since they woke me up every hour to take my "vitals." *How about instead of checking my pulse, blood pressure, and temperature, YOU JUST LET ME SLEEP?* They'd also stuck me with a needle and poured medicines right into my blood—they called it an "IV." Well, I bet *they* never tried sleeping hooked up to an IV—every time I tried to turn over, all the tubes got twisted. And if all of this wasn't enough humiliation, they put a tube in me called a catheter so I didn't have to get up to pee—and so they could keep track of it. Talk about uncomfortable. But more than anything, I was scared. Why wasn't I getting better?

I was pretty cranky the next morning when my mom

walked in. The visitor's chair-beds weren't very comfortable, so my parents decided I could handle being alone overnight and went home to sleep in their own bed. Mom took off from work the next day and came back to the hospital looking rested, showered, and well dressed (and of course carrying her ever-present cup of coffee). I looked down at my colorless hospital gown and got even crankier.

"Did you bring me some pajamas?" I asked her.

"I didn't think of it," she replied, taking a sip of her coffee.

"How about my pillow?" She shook her head no.

"Well, how about a decent breakfast?" I asked, my anger rising.

"I just wanted to get here," she said. "I wasn't thinking about anything else."

That's when Dr. Leavens walked into the room.

"Can't we get all these tubes out of me?" I demanded, gesturing to the IV. I was in a snit and no one was going to be spared.

"Emmi, we need the IV so these medicines can help make it easier for your heart to pump," Dr. Leavens explained.

"I hate this," I spat. "It's uncomfortable and annoying." I knew I was acting like a bratty five-year-old, but I didn't care. I was tired and I wanted to go home. And most of all, I was scared. What was happening to me?

"I'm sorry," she said, sounding truly apologetic.

"I'm sure you're sorry, but you aren't hooked up to this IV and stuck with this awful catheter," I said.

"No, I'm not," Dr. Leavens said. "But we're doing the best we can to take care of you."

"What about the peeing tube?" I asked. "Why can't I get up and go to the bathroom?"

"We want you to rest," Dr. Leavens answered.

"Why?" I asked.

"Emmi, you're sounding like a toddler," my mother said. "Stop asking so many questions."

"I can ask all the questions I want," I shot back at her.

"Emmi," Dr. Leavens said. "Your heart is badly damaged. We need to do all of this to save your life."

Save my life? Those words shocked me right out of my snit. Now I was totally scared; Mom saw this, came over, and took my hand.

"You mean I could die?" I said in a tiny voice. I closed my eyes.

"We'll do everything we can to make sure that doesn't happen, Emmi. Rest now," Dr. Leavens said. "I'll come back to see you later."

The booming started again and I lay back trying to breathe. *Save my life. Omigod!* I tried to stay calm and get my head to take in this new information. My mother kissed my cheek but I pushed her away—I had to think. And yet, I didn't want to think about it. *Save my life?* I just wanted to go home and have everything get back to normal. What was going to happen to me? Would I need these medicines forever? How was I going to play soccer like this? Could my heart even handle soccer?

I fell asleep for a while; when I woke up I felt a little better. I wasn't happy to be there, but I realized I needed to tow the line for a while *to save my life*. The nurses were nice on the pediatric floor, though I wondered what they really thought about always wearing scrubs with teddy bears on them.

"Your mother arranged for you to have a television," my nurse said. "Would you like me to ask if you can have a laptop?"

I smiled gratefully. "That would be nice."

It turned out the laptop was the only good thing that happened to me in the hospital. As I sat in bed waiting for my sick heart to get a little stronger, I had enough energy to write messages. I could surf some websites and e-mail Becca, and I could text with my hot chat buddy when I felt like it.

Emmi: *Day 2 and I'm going crazy.*

Sam: *So when r they letting u out?*

Emmi: *They haven't said. They keep doing tests and sending all these people in 2 talk 2 me.*

Sam: *What do they talk about?*

Emmi: *The weather.*

Emmi: *JK. They ask about my feelings and if I'm tired (duh!).*

Sam: *What do u tell them?*

Emmi: *That I'm feeling crappy and I want this to b over.*

Sam: *What do they say?*

Emmi: *That's the hard part. No 1 is saying anything. I ask questions and no 1 is answering them.*

Sam: *So give them hell. Refuse to eat or something until they answer u.*

Emmi: *Ur under the assumption that I have control here. Not at all. Not for a minute. They control my every move—and I do mean <u>every</u>.*

Ouch. I'm saying too much. Complaining too much. That's it, he's done with me.

Sam: *I looked up 'heart failure' on the web.*

Emmi: *I started 2 and then couldn't deal with it.*

Emmi: *What did u find?*

Please don't say anything bad.

Sam: *It was mostly about old people.*

Emmi: *So, Dr. Hunter, do u think I'll be ok?*

Did I really want to ask him that? And what did I think he was going to say? If he read something awful, he wouldn't tell me, would he?

Sam: *Sounds like there's a lot they can do to help u.*

That was vague, but I'll take it.

Emmi: *I guess I just have 2 b patient.*

Emmi: *Get it?*

Emmi: *Patient.*

Sam: *Cute.*

Emmi: *O. The nurse is here. Gtg.*

Sam: *ttyl*

That was awkward.

I wasn't lying, though—the nurse had walked into my room.

"Good morning, Emmi," she said. "Time to get out of bed and walk."

"I don't really feel like walking," I said. *Why are they always telling me what to do here?*

"I don't care what you feel like," she said. "The doctor says it's time to walk." The nurse was much larger than me and her crooked teeth gave her an intimidating smile, so I hung my legs over the side of the bed and got ready for a walk, putting on the robe my mother had brought me—hers. That hospital gown left me so exposed, it was good to have something to put over it to cover me, even if it was "granny" style—peachy pink, with ruffles around the neck and sleeves.

"This robe screams 'Granny,' don't you think?" I'd teased my mom as she tried to wrap it around me without dislodging the IV.

"Would you prefer that the entire hospital see your butt?" she asked.

Okay, Granny beats naked butt. I'd put the robe on. I still don't know why she couldn't have brought me a pair of decent pajamas, but at least she brought my pillow. And besides, I was trying to limit my complaining, so I didn't ask about the PJs.

The lap around the hospital floor with the nurse took a lot out of me, but I was happy to make it around once, lugging the IV pole by my side. Then I climbed back into bed and slept for an hour. Eventually I worked myself up to five or six laps, and my days were broken up by more uncomfortable tests and staff coming to talk with me. I couldn't keep track of who they were; they'd all introduce themselves as Dr. So and So, and start asking questions. Some of them examined me, and others just came in to talk.

I found out that you're never alone for long at a teaching hospital, with all these students and doctors-in-training coming and going with the senior doctors. I was getting a little nervous—okay, a lot nervous. Why couldn't they all figure this thing out, give me the medicine I needed, and let me go home to my own bed—and some privacy?

That night when Dr. Leavens came through the door, I was glad to see a familiar face. But she looked kind of . . . unhappy. It turned out she had some good news—and some that was awful.

15

They say there are moments that forever divide your life between "before" and "after." As my parents leaned against the radiator by the window holding hands—a bad sign—Dr. Leavens explained what was in store for me.

"I think you're doing very well with the medications," Dr. Leavens said to me. "And I'm going to discharge you tomorrow—you're going home."

HOORAY! I'm free. But there was more.

"I want to keep you on the IV meds," she continued. "So I'm sending you home with a pack you can wear around your waist to keep the medicines going, but letting you be a bit more mobile."

"How can I do that?" I asked. "I can't go to school with medicines around my waist."

"We're going to keep you out of school for the time being," Dr. Leavens said.

"What do you mean?" I asked. I wasn't a huge school fan, but I couldn't believe they weren't going to let me go back. I was already getting behind in my classes and I missed seeing my friends. Occasional texts and e-mails were no substitute for face-to-face contact.

"You can keep working with the tutor," my mother offered. "We don't think it'd be good for you to go through the stress of an entire school day right now."

"For how long?" I asked. "And what about soccer?"

"Soccer?" my mother exclaimed. "My God, Emmi, how can you think about soccer when you can barely walk down the hallway?"

"I walk down the hallway just fine," I replied. "Five times this morning, in fact."

"Honey, I think we have to work on getting you better before we worry about soccer," Dad said. I looked at him skeptically. He knew how important soccer was.

"Well, what do I have to do?" I asked. "What will get me better?"

There was silence in the room as all the adults just looked at me.

"What?" I asked. I looked questioningly from my mom to my dad to Dr. Leavens. Mom stood up, fidgeted, sat down, and then stood up again.

Finally, Dr. Leavens broke the silence: "Emmi, you're going to need a new heart."

16

A new heart?

With that bit of news, my current heart started beating fast and I struggled to catch my breath. My mom was by my side in a nanosecond and reached for my hand, which was good because mine started to shake so much, I needed someone to hold on to them.

How did I get to this point? A little over a month ago I was running around playing soccer; now we were talking about a new heart. I looked out the window behind Dr. Leavens and noticed it had started to snow; watching the flakes fall was hypnotizing and I allowed myself to be sucked into their rhythm.

"Emmi," Dr. Leavens said, and I turned back to the reality of what she was telling me. "Are you okay?"

"No," I stammered. "No, I'm not. Maybe my own heart'll heal—maybe it just needs more rest."

"Your heart is permanently damaged, Emmi," Dr. Leavens explained. "It's pumping blood at only a fraction of the capacity it should be. All the tests we've been doing show that it's the kind of damage that doesn't ever reverse itself—it doesn't heal. The only possibility is to give you a new heart."

"Where do you get a new heart?" I asked. "I mean, who's going to give one up for me? Doesn't everyone need their heart?"

"You'll get a donor heart. Unfortunately, someone has to die first. The good thing is that when young people tragically die in accidents, their families donate their organs. That way someone else can live, even if their child couldn't."

"Some other kid has to die so I can live?" This was too horrifying to wrap my head around. Like, how do you wish for something like that? But then, how do you not, if your own heart isn't working right?

"I know it's a scary thought," the doctor admitted.

You have no idea. After all, no one ever told *her* they'd have to hack out her heart and give her somebody else's.

"On the positive side, though, you'll be going home, and I know you've been looking forward to getting out of here," Dr. Leavens said.

"Go home to what?" I asked. "To lying in my bed and waiting for a new heart?"

My parents looked at each other, and for the first time I saw the fear and sadness in their eyes.

"Dr. Leavens said if you're feeling okay, you can go out a little sometimes," my mother said, forcing a cheerful "this isn't too bad" smile.

" 'Out a little sometimes,' " I echoed. " 'Out a little

sometimes'? This is what you want me to think is great news?" I wanted to bolt out of that room and never come back. But when you've got tubes in your arms and tubes coming out of your private parts, there's not a lot of room for running away—what Becca'd told me was my usual way of dealing with things. There was no chance of that—it was my body and I needed to accept what I was facing. I looked over at my parents and Dr. Leavens, all standing there looking genuinely concerned. But right now, I hated all three of them.

"Can you leave me alone for a while?" I asked. They looked at each other.

"Mom and I'll go get something to eat," Dad said. "And we'll check up on your brothers to see how they're doing—Aunt Mindy's with them, but it can't hurt. I mean, they're young boys and always jumping off things, so you never know. . . ." I tuned out the rest. *Keep talking, Dad. I know this isn't easy for you, either.*

"I'll see you later, Emmi," Dr. Leavens said. And they all walked out and left me by myself—just me and my horrible, damaged heart. I rolled over on my side, the one without the tubes, and started to cry. Soon my whole body was shaking with sobs.

I pictured myself running with my friends playing soccer—and I cried because I couldn't do that. I pictured school and Sam sitting two desks over in English class—and I cried because I didn't know if I'd ever figure out what was up between Sam and me. And I cried because I wouldn't be back at school for a long time—if ever. I even pictured my brothers wrestling, something that I can't stand—but I missed them and wanted to be hanging out with them more than anything.

Oh my God, I could really die. What if I never got a heart because no one had an accident? Or what if they did find a heart and it didn't work when they hooked it up to my body? What if I'm lying in my bed at home and my heart stops working—just stops? Who'd know, and even if they did, what could they do about it?

The more I thought about these things, the harder my heart pumped. I worried that I could kill myself from the stress, and I had to calm down. I tried to take deep breaths and think of something peaceful, but my mind kept rebounding back to the awful possibilities. I took more deep breaths. *Why did I send everyone away?* I needed my parents; I needed someone. Picking up the phone, I dialed Becca's cell. It started ringing, but I panicked and hung up. What was I going to tell her? How do you put all this into words? Would she still want to hang with me when I wouldn't be a whole lot of fun for who knows how long?

That's when the phone rang, jolting me out of my thoughts.

"Hello?" I said.

"Emmi, it's me," Becca said. "Did you just try to call me?"

"Yeah," I said.

"What's wrong?"

"How do you know anything's wrong?"

"Because I know," she said. I couldn't answer her—couldn't form the words. "Em? Are you still there?"

"Mmm." The tears were flowing and I just couldn't get the words out.

"I'm coming to the hospital." I could hear her rummaging around her room, getting her things together.

"You don't have to," I said, but I wanted her to come.

"My mom's working tonight. She'll drop me off on the way. I'll see you in an hour." With that, she hung up. Becca's mother was an FBI agent who worked in the city.

An hour later, my parents were back, bringing me some of the cafeteria's tomato soup that I liked. Then Becca burst through the door and ran over to my bed, kissing me on both cheeks.

"It's the European way," she explained to my parents. Our summer soccer tour had really rubbed off on her.

When my parents went home to the boys, Becca sat next to me, holding my hand. We talked about my heart for a long time, and then we talked about all the nonsense and drama going on at school. We even planned my triumphant return to soccer when this was all behind me. Then, proving she was the best of best friends, she climbed into that awful chair by the bed and stayed with me the whole night.

17

"Emmi, the nurse is here," my mother said, walking into my bedroom.

"Could you knock?" I asked.

"Can you be nicer to her than you are to me?" she replied.

I glared at her and shrugged. I knew I was being meaner to her than she deserved, but I'd already been home with the medicine pack for more than three months and there was no new heart in sight. It'd be nice to think I was one of those sweet, cheerful sick people you see on TV, but I wasn't. I was fidgety, cranky, and impatient—and scared, but trying not to think about it. Denial is a terrific coping mechanism sometimes.

The nurse, Ellen, walked into the room. She was about sixty years old and had short brown hair with a sprinkling of gray.

"How are we today?" she asked. She always asked the same questions, and in the same order. There was some comfort in how predictable she was, I guess, considering that nothing else was.

"Fine, thanks," I replied, giving her the brightest smile I could muster. No one was going to accuse me of not being nice to my nurse today.

"Is your pack giving you any trouble?" she asked.

I thought of several sarcastic replies, but thought better of it. "No."

Ellen was struggling with my hair, which kept getting caught when she was moving the IV lines around. My hair is truly awful: it's dirty blond, long, and curly, and it only looks good right after I shower. It's probably why I was so obsessed with other people's hair—hating mine so much gave me a bad case of hair envy. My mom tossed me a scrunchy, and I roped my hair into it to get it out of the way.

"I'm going to see what your brothers are doing," Mom said as she left the room.

Ellen changed the dressings on my pump; if we weren't careful, they could get infected and I'd have to be admitted to the hospital again—something I wanted to avoid at all costs.

"Are you any more tired than usual?" Ellen asked me. Usual? Which one: before-I-was-sick usual or sitting-home-all-day-half-dead usual?

"Same, I guess," I answered.

"How's your schoolwork going?" she asked.

"Fine. The tutor was here this morning. Hopefully I'm not falling too far behind." Except for socially—sometimes the gang came by, but it wasn't the same as being at school every day. A lot had happened since I'd been gone. Lauren had gone through three different boyfriends; Lauren and

Noelle had fought and made up; and I was worried Becca was going to find a new best friend.

As if she'd read my thoughts, my cell rang and it was Becca.

"Hey."

"Just checking in," she said. She called me every day on the way home from school—it'd become our routine. "How're you doing?"

"Still here." What a crazy life—any day without warning, she could call and find out that they'd found me a donor heart.

"Any good gossip?" I asked.

"Lauren dumped Marcus."

"I bet he didn't even see it coming," I said.

"They never do." We laughed; it felt good to talk about something so meaningless.

By now, Ellen had finished and gave me a wave goodbye.

"Do you think your mom'll let you go to the movies with us tonight?" Becca asked. "Everyone's going." Boy, it would be awesome to go out somewhere other than the hospital. When this all started, my mother had said I could go "out a little sometimes." So far, that'd meant one visit to my aunt's house and one trip to a specialty food store. I was due for another outing, and it'd be great to see my friends when I wasn't wearing pajamas and stuck in the house.

"I'll ask. But I still can't predict what she'll say yes or no to."

"How about the soccer game tomorrow against Nanuet?"

I'd been avoiding the spring soccer season—it'd drive me crazy to sit on the sidelines and not be able to play. Even though I loved my teammates and wanted to root for them, there was a jealous part of me that couldn't handle it, and I was angry about being sick.

"Did you see Sam today?" I was always nervous when I asked this question; I hadn't seen him since I was listed for a transplant, but he'd been a terrific chat buddy.

"Yeah, he was totally going at it with this hot blonde. The whole cafeteria was staring and when they came up for air, everyone applauded."

"Oh," I said, not sure whether to believe her—Becca could be pretty sarcastic.

"I'm joking, Em. God, don't take it so seriously. He's *just* a guy."

"No kidding."

"I guess it gives you something to do all day, if you're fantasizing about him."

"Shut up."

"I'm not the one who asks about him every day."

"And I'm not the one who followed Andy Spencer around for an entire year, hoping he'd say hello."

"That was low—and untrue."

"You're picking on a sick girl who's too tired to lift her head off the pillow each morning as she awaits her life-saving heart transplant."

"Yeah, you can't lift your head off the pillow, unless it's to text Sammy boy—I so weep for you. So do you think you're too exhausted for the movies tonight, or are you joining us? That's all I want to know right now."

"I'll ask my mom and get back to you." We hung up. There was something nice about the fact that Becca still gave me a hard time—she didn't treat me like I was sick.

I looked around my room: it was shades of pink and purple, with a pink heart border my mom put up when I was six. I loved those hearts when I was little, but now I felt like their perfection was mocking me and my damaged heart. The walls were a great shade of purple, too, and since I'd been sick, I'd made a bunch of picture collages that hung on one wall—staying home all day sure gave you different types of hobbies. My favorite collage was the one from my first soccer season, with Becca. Maybe Becca was right— maybe the only thing that got me out of bed sometimes was the possibility of texting Sam. But was that so terrible? I checked my phone and found a message there. It was a simple "Hey" and only ten minutes old. Maybe he was still there.

Emmi: *Hey, Sam.*

Sam: *Hey.*

Emmi: *sup?*

Sam: *nm u?*

Emmi: *New day, same stuff. U?*

Sam: *Ton of homework, baseball practice, the usual. Becca said she was trying 2 get u 2 the movie 2night. R u going?*

He and Becca were talking about me? That had to be good, right?

Emmi: *I hope so. U?*

Sam: *Is it 2 much 4 u?*

78

Emmi: *I feel good today. Thanks 4 asking. I need 2 ask the jailers if they'll spring me for the nite.*

Sam: *Well, may b I'll c u there. Bowling alley gave me the nite off.*

Emmi: *What's the occasion?*

Sam: *Another guy needed Saturday off. Traded shifts.*

Emmi: *Cool. C u. g2g.*

I begged my mother to go—down on one knee kind of begging—and shockingly, she said yes. I texted Becca.

Emmi: *Hey, Bec, u there?*

Becca: *yeah, 'sup?*

Emmi: *I will definitely b at the movies. When r u picking me up?!!!*

18

I'd be lying if I said I wasn't nervous about the movies. First of all, I hadn't seen most of my friends since this whole thing happened. And I'm sure I didn't look great—I'd lost weight, I was deathly pale, and my hair—well, it was never great even on a good day. I must have tried on seven outfits, but nothing goes with a medicine pump.

"Let's go already. They'll sell out and it won't matter what you're wearing." Becca, who sat on my bed, didn't have a lot of patience for clothing and stuff. As much as I liked soccer and lived in sweats, I liked to look good sometimes, too. It was easier for Becca—she looked great no matter what she wore. Tall and thin's a lot easier than short and athletic with knotty hair. "I haven't seen Sam in months. I want to make a good reimpression."

"A reimpression?"

"Well, I can't make a first impression—he already knows me. So this is my reimpression." Becca rolled her eyes and continued to push me out the door.

We got to the movies to find the usual Friday night

scene. There isn't a lot to do in New City on Friday nights, so we wait for a new movie to come out and then it's the biggest deal in town. Half of our school must have been there, and we saw huge clusters of girls and guys. The girls were mostly dressed the same: tight jeans, trendy sneakers, layered tops, too much makeup. They all had the same long straight hair and they walked in packs, whispering and giggling. The guys were trying to look cool, sometimes by punching each other. I'm sure nobody would be surprised to find out that the movie theater workers hate Friday nights.

Becca and I bought our tickets and managed to find Lauren and Noelle who had saved us two seats.

"Nice of you to join us," Lauren said.

"You try getting dressed with a medicine pump strapped around your waist," I said. Hearing this, the girl in front of me turned around to stare. I realized it was Jenny, who sat in front of me in English class.

"Hi, Jenny," I said.

"Oh, hi, Emmi. Umm, how're you doing?" Jenny said, looking everywhere but right at me.

"I'm good. How's Mr. Mistretta's class?"

"Well, you know, he makes us work hard and everything, but, well, um, you're really not missing anything." She obviously was uncomfortable talking to me.

"I'm doing the work at home with a tutor," I told her.

"Oh, well, that's good," Jenny said and looked down at her hands.

I had to let her off the hook. "I'm going to get some popcorn now," I said.

"Talk to you later." Jenny turned around in her seat with an audible sigh of relief.

"You guys want any popcorn?" I asked my friends.

"No, we snuck in our own candy," Lauren answered. "Remember, we hate paying all that money for fifty cents worth of popcorn? You haven't been away that long, have you?"

"I guess being caught up in life-or-death issues distracted me a little—sorry." I grabbed my bag and went to the concession stand. A few people I knew from school said hi; I thought I saw some girls pointing at me and whispering, but I was trying not to be paranoid. I scanned the theater for Sam, but I didn't find him. My mood sank, thinking he wasn't coming as I stood on line and watched everyone. Groups of girls chatted and the line moved slowly as the pimply kid behind the counter salted the vat of newly popped popcorn. Salt—damn. That's on my "restricted list." When you have heart failure, they want you to cut down on your salt intake so you don't retain water. But what was the point of being at the movies if I couldn't even have popcorn? This really sucked. I bought myself some Raisinets and a bottle of water and went back to my seat.

Our group had moved to different seats. "While you were gone, a girl with a horrible cold sat next to us, so we moved. We knew you shouldn't be exposed to that," Noelle said as I sat down. She was right—if I got a bad cold or infection, I'd be temporarily taken off the transplant list. I guess even coming to the movies had its risks, but I didn't want to think about my heart right now. I just wanted to enjoy being a normal sixteen-year-old for a few hours, even if I couldn't sit there and munch on some popcorn. I scanned the theater once more, trying to spot Sam.

"Oooh, Emmi, give me some of your Raisinets," Lauren said. "I love Raisinets. They're actually pretty healthy—they've got fruit in them."

"Shriveled grapes covered in chocolate cannot be considered healthy," Becca shot back.

"Look, the label says '40% Less Fat,' " Lauren insisted.

"It's candy, moron. Rationalize it all you want—it's still going straight to your hips," Becca said. Nothing ever went straight to Becca's hips—not ever. She could eat half a cheesecake every day for lunch and still be model thin. I looked at my own hips. Now I couldn't have popcorn, and I didn't want the Raisinets anymore either. I opened up the water bottle and sat back into my seat.

The theater darkened completely and the previews began. I couldn't help looking back at the door; it opened twice, but it wasn't Sam. Oh well—I settled in and watched the movie, disappointed big-time. Ninety minutes, one popcorn fight, and two kids getting kicked out the theater later, the lights came back on; but still no sign of Sam. We got up and started leaving the theater.

"Emmi," someone said. I turned to see Sam. He was here after all!

"Hey," I said, wondering what he was thinking and how I looked. "I didn't see you before."

"We came in a few minutes late."

"You didn't miss much," I said.

"You look great," he said and smiled. I had forgotten how much I liked his smile—and his body. Wow.

"Thanks. You know, when you're home all day, there's lots of time to devote to personal hygiene." Yikes, was that too stupid to say, or what?

"Well, in a weird way, it suits you. I mean, not that you look good sick, just that . . . well, you look good." We were both struggling with this face-to-face thing. It's much easier to text—gives you time to think about what you're saying before you actually say it.

"Better than you expected, right?" I tried to get him out of it.

"Yeah, I guess I was picturing you with giant circles under your eyes and tubes coming out all over and your hair all wild and sticking up."

He was picturing me!

"Glad I brushed my hair today, just to prove you wrong."

"Listen, I know you can't get out much, but maybe I could come over or something. I can help you go over the stuff you're missing in class."

"That'd be great." I smiled my biggest dimple smile and was rewarded with another one of his eye-lighting grins.

"Sam, we gotta go," his friend shouted as he stood halfway out the theater door.

"I better run," he said, leaning over to give me a kiss on the cheek. "It's great to see you." And with that, he was gone.

I'd say this was worth every bit of begging I'd done to get my parents to let me go out tonight!

19

Despite how great it felt to do something normal, and especially to see Sam, the movies took a lot out of me. I felt lousy all weekend, and I slept a lot more than usual. Not only that, but my ankles were swollen and puffy, and my sweatpants felt too small. Now, it's one thing when that happens with your jeans, but sweats? It's a little scary when even an elastic waist gets too tight.

"Water weight gain is common with congestive heart failure," Dr. Leavens explained at my appointment on Monday. I guess at least I could blame it on that instead of sitting around all day and not playing soccer.

"Did I do anything wrong to make this happen?" I asked. Maybe I shouldn't have gone to the movies, and I hoped my mother wouldn't jump on that with an "I told you so."

"Not necessarily. Let's increase your Lasix dose and see if we can get some of that water out of you," she suggested.

"The Lasix made me very thirsty last time," I complained.

"That's normal. I know it's a little bit uncomfortable, but it's important to get rid of the excess water. Anything else on your mind?" She looked at me, but she also glanced over at my parents.

Gee, where to start?

But we all had the Big Question on our minds: When would a heart become available? My mom started to speak but stopped herself. I looked over at my dad, who'd turned to face Dr. Leavens. "Do we have any idea where she is on the list? Or how long it might be?" There, he said what we were all wondering.

"Well, you never can predict these things. As I've told you before, Emmi's now considered a 1B, which means she's a high priority. The only category higher is a 1A, and thankfully, she isn't sick enough for that yet. Hopefully the heart will come before she ever gets to that point. But the good news is that her blood type is B, and for some reason, B's tend to get hearts sooner."

Then she turned to me. "Emmi, all we can do is make sure you're taking your meds and not exerting yourself too much. Other than that, we wait."

But sixteen-year-olds are not good at waiting. I was tired, I was bored, and I was scared. Dr. Leavens started to examine me, and for what felt like the millionth time in the last few months, I let her listen to my heart and take my blood pressure. But the tighter the blood pressure cuff got, the more trapped I felt. As it squeezed my arm tighter and tighter, I wanted to rip it off and run out of the room.

I would've gone anywhere, just to make everything go back to normal.

20

I checked my hair in the mirror for the fifth time in ten minutes: yep, still awful. And I was really pale—I put a small amount of blush on my cheeks and rubbed it in. Still pale.

Sam was coming over. He'd be here any minute. Did I look okay?

I put on a little more lip gloss, and then I wiped it off. I didn't want to look overly made up, like I was trying too hard. Then the doorbell rang. My heart did its BOOM, BOOM, BOOM thing, but this time for a different reason. Why was I so nervous? We texted all the time—how different could this be?

My brother Eli ran to the door and opened it, and then he screamed, "EMMI! Company!"

I walked down the stairs to find Sam in my front hallway. Deep breath, big smile—as dimpled as possible.

"Hi," I said, smiling at him. He smiled back and our eyes held.

How was I going to focus on math?

"Let's go into the dining room where we'll have room to work," I said. We set out our books, said polite hellos to my parents when they came in the room, and then started in on the math. My parents went into the kitchen with Eli.

"Okay, problem one," I said, picking up my pencil and looking at the math book. Sam moved his chair a little closer and I almost lost my breath.

"Problem one," he said. I turned as he said it and he leaned over and kissed me. The kiss lasted a wonderful few minutes. Then I pulled away and turned toward the book.

"Problem one," I repeated. Who was I kidding? I turned back and kissed him again. This was a great way to do homework!

"I don't hear any math going on out there," Eli shouted through the door.

"Eli!" I heard my father say. Sam and I laughed and turned back to the books.

It took us a lot of time to get through our homework.

21

Emmi: *Hey.*

Becca: *Hey. 'sup?*

Emmi: *Thinking about dying. U?*

Becca: *ha ha.*

Becca: *Em? u there?*

Emmi: *Where would I b? I have nowhere else 2 b. Just here, all day.*

Becca: *u r not going to die.*

Emmi: *How do u know? They could find a heart, do the surgery, and the new heart might not start. Or I could have the new heart for a few weeks and my body could reject it. Or they may never even find a heart in time.*

Becca: *Or u could be fine.*

Emmi: *I've been waiting almost 4 months. Every day I wake up and think this will be the day. And it never is. Some people wait 4 years. I don't have years—I'm not going to* *be 16 forever. I want to be a nomal person and do all the normal things. The whole spring soccer season is almost gone.*

Becca: *So u'll be there 4 the fall.*

Emmi: *Bec, do you believe in an afterlife?*

Becca: *I don't know. Some of the guys my mom has arrested deserve to go to hell, so I kind of hope that hell exists. But is there a heaven? I don't know. What do u think?*

Emmi: *When my Grandma Josie died I imagined her reuniting with her mother and father. She missed them so much and I liked the idea that she was with them again and happy.*

Becca: *U r not going to die, Em. It'll be a long time b4 u can c your grandma again.*

Emmi: *I don't know, sometimes I wonder…*

Becca: *Stop thinking that way. What r u doing later? Can I come over?*

Emmi: *Actually, Sam's coming over to study.*

Becca: *Isn't that the 3rd time this week?*

Emmi: *4th. But who's counting?!*

Becca: *How much studying are you actually doing?*

Emmi: *Lots.*

Becca: *Yeah, right.*

Emmi: *Well, some.*

Becca: *I want details!*

Emmi: *Unlike SOME people, I don't kiss and tell.*

Becca: *I'm ignoring that. Don't forget our Pact about not having sex.*

Emmi: *I'm a good girl.*

Becca: *I trust u. It's our little baseball player I'm not so sure of.*

22

"Have you ever read *Romeo and Juliet*?" We were studying in the dining room when Sam asked me that. I bet he was the first baseball player from North Village High who ever asked any girl that question.

"Sure. In ninth-grade English. Why?"

"Well, someone made a comment about it yesterday, saying we.were like Romeo and Juliet," he said.

"Yeah, but they were totally different. Their families were feuding and didn't want them getting together." I didn't like where this was heading. Did he think I was going to die? Was that what was on his mind?

I got up to go to the bathroom—again. Whenever I get my Lasix dose, I do laps back and forth to the bathroom. But at least my jeans were fitting again, so I guess it was working. When I came back, I sat next to Sam.

"Do you think I'm going to die?"

"No!"

"Then why were you talking about Romeo and Juliet?" I was getting agitated.

"No reason, Em. It was stupid. Forget it and let's look at the math."

"Romeo kills himself because he thinks Juliet's dead."

"Em, I didn't mean anything by it—really. Just never mind about it, okay?"

He pulled out his math book and started to do one of the problems. I slammed my book shut.

"Listen, you've been coming over every other night and it's great, but if something's on your mind, you have to tell me."

He looked down at his textbook and flipped through the pages. "I worry about you sometimes. More than sometimes—a lot." He looked at me with those green and gold eyes, then leaned over and kissed me, a really good, long kiss. We kissed for a few minutes, and for the first time all day, I wasn't worried about my heart.

But then the strangest sound broke the silence around us. At first I wasn't sure what it was. But then I realized it was the beeper the hospital gave us—the one that would tell us there was a heart available.

I jumped up and screamed, running into the kitchen with the beeper.

"What is it?" Sam asked, following me.

"My hospital beeper!"

My mother came running in; she picked up the beeper, her hands shaking.

"Call!" I handed her the phone. By this time, my brothers had come up from the basement and we all stood around my mother, who was holding the phone. Then she handed

95

me the beeper and I read the numbers out as she pressed each button. But she messed up and had to start over. Jeremy and Eli started punching each other and I kicked Jeremy—hard.

"Ouch, Em. Why me?" He went to kick me back.

"Can you two stop it for one minute?" I shouted. I couldn't believe they were doing this now, of all times.

"Boys, go back to the basement," my mother reprimanded. But nobody moved and then the call connected.

"Yes, this is Mrs. Miller, Emmi's mother. Our beeper just went off." All eyes were on Mom and I leaned in close to the phone to hear what was being said. Sam took my hand, and I took in a deep breath and listened.

"Mrs. Miller, this is Nancy Jones, the transplant coordinator at Children's. We think we've found a heart for Emmi." I exhaled. "Can you come right in? The heart's coming from Albany, so we need you here as soon as possible." I couldn't move and felt frozen to the floor.

"We're on our way," Mom said and hung up the phone, then started to dial my father's cell.

"Omigod." I was numb. I thought I'd be more scared, but instead I didn't feel anything.

"Jeremy, get Emmi's overnight bag from her room," my mom said.

"And my pillow," I added, stepping into my flip-flops.

"Let me call Aunt Mindy," Mom said. She's my mom's younger sister who lived nearby.

"Mrs. Miller, I'll stay with these guys until she gets here if you want," Sam offered.

"Yes!" A cheer went up from my brothers. Jeremy and Eli thought Sam was awesome and would make him run football plays or play catch in the basement whenever we hung with them.

"Omigod," I repeated. Sam put his big arms around me for a minute and I relaxed against him.

"C'mon, Em. We have to get moving," my mother said, grabbing her pocketbook and travel coffee mug. She took my duffle bag from my hand and I pulled myself away from Sam, reluctant to leave him and face what was ahead.

"Good luck," he whispered to me. I drank in his green-gold eyes for what could be the last time, then walked toward the door and saw Eli jump on Sam's back. Jeremy looked at me and waved good luck. At twelve, he understood a lot more than little Eli.

Mom and I got into our minivan and we headed down the Palisades Parkway in silence. It was warm for April, but I couldn't stop shivering. But even as nervous as I was, my mind kept wandering back to Sam and that kiss. And then I'd remember where we were going and my brain would snap back to pondering my new heart.

"Your father's meeting us there—he's probably almost there by now." Dad's office was not very far from the hospital, probably around seven and a half miles, and Mom was zigzagging around slow-moving cars.

"Mom, you're going too fast." I was jittery enough already without us weaving like that.

"It's a forty-minute ride without traffic, but it's rush hour—what if we hit traffic? We might not get there in time." That made me even more nervous. And she went on: "Mindy can't get there until eight, and I forgot to tell Sam to give the boys dinner. Do you think he'll think to feed them something? Should I call them?"

"I don't think Jeremy or Eli will let him forget about dinner. I'm sure he'll order a pizza or something."

"You don't think they'll try to cook something instead? Can Sam cook? Does he know how to use a stove?" She took a sip of coffee and it spilled into the cup holder as she put it back.

"I'm sure he's microwaved a frozen dinner before. Don't worry, they'll be fine—he'll figure something out."

Here I was, calming my mom down. Shouldn't it be the other way around? Meanwhile, she whizzed around a white Corvette and flew past a Porsche. She's the crazy lady in a minivan, but before we knew it, the George Washington Bridge was in sight. She sped through the EZ Pass lanes and we both breathed a sigh of relief to find very little traffic on the bridge. About halfway across, we could see the hospital come into view. I couldn't take my eyes off the big brick building where I was going to get a new heart—and a new life.

23

We made it safely to the hospital, where the automatic doors opened and we were greeted by a blast of air-conditioned air. Mom took my hand, something I didn't usually let her do—it's too embarrassing at my age. But with all that was happening, it was nice. Her hand was warm and soft, and it made me feel like she was taking care of me.

Soon we crowded into an elevator and I stood in the back, pushed against the wall, studying all the people. Some were doctors, looking official with white coats and badges; others must have been patients and their parents. A baby was crying and his mother was trying to get him to stop by bouncing him up and down. She tried to stick a pacifier into his mouth, but the kid was having none of it. I was so caught up in watching to see whether he'd stop crying, I didn't notice when we arrived at our floor.

We got off the elevator and faced the Pediatric Cardiology Center, and then I couldn't move. My feet were glued to the floor, even though I saw my father smiling at me from the brightly colored nurse's stand. Mom walked toward my father, but I was still stuck in that same spot. Mom looked back and told me to come on, but when I tried to move, I still couldn't—like I was wearing two giant cement shoes that were too heavy to budge.

"I— I—" I could barely speak. My father noticed and came over to me, then put his arm around me and walked me to a metal chair in the waiting room. My legs wobbled and I collapsed into the chair with a thud.

"I'm trying to be brave," I blurted and then the tears started falling. My whole face was wet and I'm sure my nose was bright red, but I couldn't stop. Then the woman sitting next to me handed me a box of tissues. I took one out and blew my nose. Who was I kidding? I wasn't brave at all—I was scared out of my mind, and who wouldn't be? I mean, I could die! At that thought, the flood of tears resumed.

A kid about eight sat across from me; he had a Nintendo DS and was totally focused on it. What was he doing here, and how could he be so relaxed? Across the room, a two-year-old ran around in circles, clearly oblivious to whatever it was that'd brought her here. I wished I could be like that.

"I'm going to check on your mom and the paperwork," my dad said. "Are you okay by yourself for a few minutes?" I nodded and started pulling apart the tissue in my hand, tearing it into as many tiny pieces as possible. I was so intent on destroying it that I didn't notice the guy sitting next to me on the other side.

"I think you've thoroughly obliterated the tissue," he

said. I looked up and saw a guy about my age. He was skinny and cute in a sort of nerdy way. His brown hair was cut spiky, and his small oval glasses made him look wise. He was wearing a FLEETWOOD MAC concert T-shirt—an unusual choice for a teenage boy. They were old, and more my parents' thing.

"Hi, I'm Abe," he said. "Are you okay?"

I shrugged.

"I had a transplant two years ago today—it's my anniversary."

"Two years?" I repeated. He looked good—normal, almost.

"So why are you here?" Abe asked.

"Viral myocarditis."

"Transplant?" he asked.

"Today," I said, in barely a whisper. "Like right now."

"I was pretty scared when I was having mine, but it was all right. And look—here I am, two years later!" he said, raising his arms in victory. "It hurts right after the surgery, so let them give you pain meds. And they'll give you a pillow to press against your chest—your sternum. But after a few days it's not so bad. And you get this cool souvenir chest scar," he said, pulling up his shirt to show off the scar running the length of his rib cage.

"Too Much Information! Pull your shirt back down," I said, laughing.

"After the surgery, you can show me yours!" he said, wiggling his eyebrows and winking.

"Emmi, they're ready for you," my mother broke in.

My father walked over to me and helped me stand up. I had a bit more feeling in my legs now and was able to cross the room without freezing up this time. Before we walked away, Abe ran over and handed me a small blue slip of paper.

"My phone number and my e-mail. In case you want to talk."

"Thanks." I smiled at him. My sweats and T-shirt had no pockets, so I gave the note to my mom, who put it into her handbag. Abe seemed so upbeat and positive. I wondered how he was the day of his transplant.

"The team's just arrived in Albany to look at the heart," my mother said, updating us. "While we wait, they'll run some tests on Emmi before she goes to surgery."

A nurse walked us toward the exam area—a tiny blonde with the straightest, most beautiful hair I'd ever seen. I followed her hair down the hall until she opened a door into a sterile-looking exam room with a sink, two chairs, and an exam table covered in white paper. Then she handed me a cloth hospital gown washed so many times it was almost colorless.

"Put it on with the opening in the front," she instructed.

"Can I keep my underwear on?" I asked.

"Yes, but take off everything else." The nurse left with my dad while I got undressed. My mom watched me kick off my flip-flops and shed my T-shirt and sweats. My bra was last, and I looked down at my tiny chest: having small boobs was fine for soccer, but sometimes I wished I was bigger.

"It'd be better with big breasts," I said. "Then the scar wouldn't show as much."

My mom kept looking at me, and every few seconds, she tucked her hair behind her ears. It was making me nervous and I started thinking about the surgery.

"Don't make me start to cry again," I warned.

"Sorry," she said and looked away.

Then the door opened and Dr. Leavens appeared, with my dad right behind her. "Are you ready, Emmi?" she asked.

"No. But we're doing it anyway, right?" I smiled, trying to look more relaxed than I felt.

The door opened again, and an athletic looking doctor with dirty blond hair and the same green-gold eyes as Sam walked in.

"Emmi, this is Dr. Harrison. He's going to be your surgeon," Dr. Leavens said. Dr. Harrison smiled at me and he even had Sam's smile. I liked this guy already.

"Hi, Emmi. How are you?"

"Scared out of my mind. You?"

He nodded and said, "Well, I do this kind of thing all the time, so I'm feeling pretty good, thanks." Another smile made me feel a bit more relaxed.

"Here's what's going to happen," he said. "We're going to get you on a gurney and set up your IV. Then we'll put a tranquilizer in the IV to help you relax. Then, when you're nice and relaxed, we'll wheel you into the operating room. Our transplant team is waiting to get you ready for your part of the surgery, and another part of the team is up in

Albany to see the heart and make sure that it's a good match for you. We won't put you under the anesthesia until we're sure the donor heart's perfect."

"You mean it's not okay sometimes?" I asked. What did he mean?

"Sometimes. But that very rarely happens," he said. "We don't want to give you a heart if it isn't going to help you."

Was he kidding me? This might not happen, after all this? I didn't know what scared me more—it happening, or it *not* happening.

"Why wouldn't the heart be good enough?" I wanted to know more.

"There're several reasons. It could be enlarged, or it could have arteries that aren't working well, or it could have a defect no one knew about before."

"Then what?"

"We'll wait for another heart. But Emmi, I don't think that's going to be the case. I think you're going to go to sleep and wake up with a healthy new heart. And then you're going to feel so much better."

But my mind was racing. *What if I don't wake up? What if I do wake up, but it's so painful I can't take it?*

"Abe—the guy I met in the waiting room—says it hurts a lot after the surgery."

"Abe's right. It can hurt. But I've had other patients who've been surprised that it didn't hurt as much as they expected. We have great doctors here who are very good at managing pain after surgery."

Pain meds are good. I can deal with pain meds.

The nurse came back into the room carrying a tray with a bunch of needles and tubes. I used to be afraid of having my blood drawn, but by now I'd been poked so many times, I barely noticed.

"Honey, I'm going to take a little blood." The blonde had a sweet, southern drawl, and she expertly drew my blood and started filling the vials. "Are you okay?" she asked.

Not really, but I nodded.

"We're going to go call and see what's going on up in Albany," Dr. Leavens explained and she and Dr. Harrison left the room. My nurse took my blood pressure and temperature, and weighed me. And then it was time to wait.

My parents sat on the chairs and I hopped up onto the exam table. It was a little chilly in the room, particularly in that flimsy hospital gown. None of us had anything to read, and none of us felt like talking or even knew what to say. So we sat in silence for a while. I heard my father's stomach rumble and realized that dinnertime had come and gone.

"Dad, why don't you get something to eat?"

"No, I want to be here when they take you into the OR," he said. *Omigod—I'm going to the OR. The Operating Room—where they'll operate on me. They're going to cut me open and—* I couldn't think about it anymore.

"Why is it taking so long?" I demanded.

"I don't know," my mother said, and then she got up, opened the exam room door, and peeked out to find someone to ask. The hallway was empty and she came back in and closed the door.

"I spoke to Aunt Mindy—she's at the house now. It wasn't fair for Sam to have to stay all night," my mom said.

"I'm sure he wouldn't mind," I said, trying to grasp on to the memory of Sam's kiss. If I thought about Sam and how cute he was, and how nice his kisses were, maybe I could avoid thinking about the scary stuff—the stuff that was about to happen.

"But his mother might not like it, since there's school tomorrow."

Oh yeah, I forgot about school.

"It sounded like the boys had a fun night," she continued. "And Sam gave them dinner—he found microwave dinners in the freezer."

"I knew he'd figure it out." When Sam smiled at me, nothing else mattered. I even loved the way his top teeth overlapped a little. *Will I ever get to see those teeth again?* I wanted him to hold me and tell me I'd be okay.

My father's stomach growled again and he looked down at his watch. I felt bad—he looked so uncomfortable in his suit and dress shoes. Not that I felt so comfortable in my hospital gown. Mom started pacing, and then the door opened and we all looked up.

It was Dr. Harrison, and there was no smile in his eyes.

"It's not good news from Albany: the heart was enlarged, and we don't want to transplant Emmi with anything less than a perfect heart. We had to turn it down."

"No!" I exclaimed, shocked. "No!" *How can they do this to me? I need a new heart and they told me there was a heart. And now there isn't. They turned it down.*

106

"I'm sorry, Emmi." He looked truly sad.

"But I was all ready. I'm here and they took my blood. And I have this silly gown on. It's not fair!"

"I know it's not fair, but there's nothing we can do about it. Hopefully another heart will be available soon."

"So we just go home and wait some more? I'm *sick* of waiting. I want to do it now, and get it over with!" I was being unreasonable, but I didn't care. My mom took my hand but I yanked it away.

"Get dressed, Emmi, and we'll have some dinner and go home." She handed me my clothes and I snatched them from her.

"Can you get out of here so I can change?"

"She's disappointed," my mother said to Dr. Harrison and my father.

"Of course I'm disappointed. I want to get this behind me and go on with my life. You don't know what it's like to wait and to think it's going to happen—and it doesn't! Just leave me alone so I can change, and then we can get the hell out of here."

The adults all left the room, and I started shaking. I kicked the exam table with my best soccer kick: Ouch!

This totally sucked.

24

By the time we left the hospital it was ten p.m. I was exhausted and overwhelmed by all the emotions I'd gone through that day, but most of all I was angry. How did they expect me to go from getting the call and preparing myself for the transplant and being scared I was going to die, only to have it canceled at the last minute and *then* have to try and go back to the long, boring wait after such a huge buildup? Why couldn't they figure out if they had a good heart *before* calling me in and getting my hopes up? It was such a stupid system.

We found a sushi place that was still open and went in for takeout. "Get me the sushi super deluxe," I demanded. It was the most expensive thing on the menu, but tonight I didn't care. Dr. Leavens said I wouldn't be able to have sushi after my transplant (there was a danger of the bacteria contaminating the new heart), so I may as well enjoy it now.

"Should we get some for Jeremy? He's become a sushi addict," my mother wondered. My brother ate nothing but chicken nuggets and hot dogs until he was eleven, but then he discovered he liked sushi and couldn't get enough of it now.

"Won't he be asleep?" my father asked.

"I spoke to Mindy—she said the boys were waiting up for us."

We picked up our order and headed back to the car. When we got home and walked into the house, Jeremy and Eli were in their usual spots in front of the TV with a Yankee game on. But Eli was fast asleep on the couch.

"He was trying so hard to stay up to see you, but he conked out a few minutes ago," Aunt Mindy explained. She was ten years younger than my mother and taught English at my high school. Luckily she was cool and the kids all liked her; it would have been embarrassing if she were mean or weird or worse.

My father picked up Eli and carried him up the stairs to his room. I went into the kitchen to eat my sushi and Jeremy was right behind me.

"Em, you okay?" Jeremy asked.

"No."

He looked at me with the sweetest look of concern. Even though we fight a lot, deep down, I know he's a good kid.

"I was kind of worried about you—you know, if everything would go okay."

"Wow, didn't know you cared."

"Of course I care. You're my big sister. I may act like a pain in the butt sometimes, but I actually like you. Pissing you off is just a hobby with me."

"Jem, that's sweet. Maybe you could find a different hobby, though—one that doesn't make me feel the need to beat the crap out of you on a daily basis."

"I'll look into it," he said, trying not to laugh.

"Want some sushi?"

"I thought you'd never ask!"

"Were you just being nice to me to get some of my food?"

"Me? Do that? Never." He smiled at me, then said, "I'm sorry it didn't happen tonight."

"Me, too."

"Sam left a message for you."

"Really? What?"

"I think it went: kissy, kissy, huggy, huggy."

"Shut up!" I said, throwing a piece of yellowtail at him.

25

"So what d'you want to be when you grow up?" Sam asked me one night when we were studying on my family room couch. Sam's visits had become pretty regular; mostly we studied, but sometimes the study sessions dissolved into make-out sessions (when my brothers weren't around to police us, that is). It all seemed pretty genuine, and I'd long ago stopped worrying about Brian's warning that Sam was a player.

"You're assuming I'm going to live through all of this," I answered.

"Yeah, of course I'm assuming that. Aren't you?"

"Sometimes. Most of the time. Oh, I don't know."

"Let's assume this is going to be over soon and you're going to live." He took my hand and held it in his.

"Okay," I agreed, moving a book aside and sitting closer to him.

"What do you think you want to do?" he repeated, slowly tracing each of my fingers. I was getting distracted and couldn't think straight about my answer.

"I don't know. After I play soccer in college, maybe I'll play pro for a while. Then I think I'd like to do something in another country. Like maybe teach kids to speak English in Mongolia. Or do a Peace Corps kind of thing. How about you?" I looked up at him. God, was he gorgeous.

"Well, when I was nine I thought I'd play for the Yankees." He smiled and batted a pretend ball out of the park.

"Yeah, you and every other nine-year-old—just ask Jeremy. He's twelve and still has that dream. And what about now—that you're more realistic?" I put my head on his shoulder, snuggling close.

"I know what I *don't* want to do," he said.

"What's that?"

"Anything to do with making money for somebody else. I don't get how my dad does it every day. He wakes up, puts on a suit and tie, and gets stressed out about investing all this money that's not even his. And at the end of the day, he comes home and it's late, and he's missed everything. And all he's accomplished is making someone else more money. He hasn't helped anyone or performed a service or anything."

"Yeah, I know what you mean—my dad's a lawyer for big corporations. He keeps saying he's going to leave it and teach law school, or else work for some environmental group. But he's kind of stuck doing the corporate stuff until we're all done with college."

"Maybe I'll come with you to Mongolia," Sam said.

"I'd like that." Sam leaned down to kiss me. Boy, this

certainly made studying a lot more fun. I wondered how long Sam would be content with just making out, though.

Sam pushed me down gently and we were lying side by side on the couch. He was crushing my English homework and I hoped Mr. Mistretta wouldn't mind. As we were kissing, I slid the rest of the books and papers off the couch to prevent any further damage, and Sam ran his hand from my neck to my shoulder and down the length of my arm to my hand. One by one, he kissed each finger and I felt so good. Then he kissed my lips and climbed on top of me.

"Careful! My meds!" I shouted.

"Omigod. I'm so sorry," he said, jumping up.

"No—it's fine," I said, kissing him again. We remained that way, sitting up and kissing for a while. I slid my hands over his neck and his ear and he moaned; he slid his hand under my T-shirt, but I grabbed it.

"What? Why?" he asked. "I'll be careful about the medicine pack."

"No. It's not that."

"Are you scared? Because of your heart?"

"Yes. But no, that's not it."

"Then what?"

"You need to know something."

"I wasn't trying to—"

"You weren't now, maybe, but . . ."

"Emmi, what's wrong?"

"I'm not going to sleep with you, Sam."

He paused. "I wasn't thinking about that. Especially with your medicines and your heart and all. But maybe you could ask Dr. Leavens—she seems pretty cool."

"It's not just that. I made a pact with Becca—we're going to wait."

"Wait for what?" He was sitting up straight now and had pulled away from me.

"Marriage—or at least engagement. Or maybe being deeply in love. But it's not going to be in high school."

"What about all those European guys you two are always joking about?" he asked.

"We were just making out—and flirting a lot."

"They must've hated you."

"Maybe, but I didn't really care."

"Wow." He moved away from me even farther. "Why?"

"Is that the only reason you want to be with me?" I asked.

"No. But I kinda thought, well, I knew it wouldn't be now, but I thought it would be—I just assumed, well, I really like you and—"

"I feel like I'm too young. And I can't risk getting pregnant. I've always felt this way. And the whole heart thing makes it a lot worse."

"Okay," he said, getting off the couch.

What does he mean? "Okay, I get it and respect you"? Or "okay, this is not for me anymore"? What was actually happening here?

He gathered his books, separating mine from his. I watched him and I started putting my things into a pile next to his. We continued like this for about a minute in silence; it was a very long minute. When all of his things were together, he stuffed them into his backpack and stood up, throwing the backpack over his shoulder. I walked him to the door and he opened it.

"I don't get it," I said to him. "Is that what it's all been about? Did you think it would be cool to do it with the sick girl?" He looked at me, and for a second I thought he was going to smile and say he was kidding. But he didn't.

"No. That's not it. But"—he looked at me with a mixture of passion and disappointment—"I just need some space, I think." Then he walked out the door.

I watched him go to his car, head bowed and studying the grass. I just couldn't believe it. I thought this guy was different—that he liked me for me, not for what he was hoping to get. It was just like Matt Stenwick, pushing things too far. What was it with guys?

I felt so stupid. Was this the guy who wanted to be my "chat buddy" all these months? The one who seemed to like hanging with me as much as he liked kissing me?

I sat down on the couch, but then jumped back up—it was too much like being at the scene of the crime. I went into the kitchen and knocked over a chair, but I didn't care. The sobs started coming and I couldn't stop them. I dragged myself upstairs to my room and turned on my computer; maybe I could catch Becca or someone online. Sure enough, Becca was there.

Emmi: *Bec, r u there?*
Becca: *sup?*
Emmi: *I think I just blew it.*
Becca: *What?*

Emmi: *Our stupid no-sex pact.*

Becca: *What did u do?*

Emmi: *It's what I didn't do.*

Becca: *There's nothing wrong with our pact. If he likes u, it shouldn't matter, remember?*

Emmi: *I didn't think it would. And it never did b4. But it does now. It matters.*

Becca: *What happened? I can't believe u r folding on this.*

Emmi: *Maybe u just haven't met anyone yet that meant enough 2 u?*

Becca: *Maybe u r being 2 blind 2C what it's all about?*

Emmi: *What's it all about? Losing a great guy over some stupid pact?*

Becca: *I'm not going 2 fight with u about this.*

Emmi: *Fine. Bye.*

This user had signed off.

26

I couldn't sleep and kept going through the whole thing again in my brain: the pact seemed so logical, so honorable—up until now. It used to feel like we were taking charge of our bodies and everything, but now I'd lost Sam over it and I wondered if it was really that important. And maybe part of me really wanted to be with him in that way. But Brian was right: Sam was a player. And he'd certainly played me.

The next day I tried to do my schoolwork but could barely concentrate. I must have read the same passage of *The Crucible* about fifteen times. I couldn't even bring myself to shower or change my clothes—I was so down.

My brothers had been at school all day and my mom had been at work; usually when they all came home, I was so happy for human contact, I greeted them at the door. But today I didn't even answer their hellos.

Noticing the change, my mom poked her head into my room. "You okay?"

"Fine." If I gave her a one-word answer and nothing more, maybe she'd leave me alone.

"Are you in pain? Is something wrong?" She wasn't going to let me off that easy.

"It has nothing to do with my heart. But I'd appreciate it if you'd leave—now." But instead she came into the room.

"I said *leave.*"

"Emmi—"

"Mom. I'm fine. I'm trying to get my work done, so leave me alone, okay?" We both knew she wasn't buying the schoolwork thing, but realizing she wasn't getting anywhere with me, she walked out of the room. Good. I wasn't in the mood for any of her speeches and I wasn't about to say anything about what'd happened with Sam—she wouldn't understand anyway.

Then my cell rang—it was Becca. I opened and shut it without talking. It rang again. "What?" I snapped into the phone.

"I was calling to see how you were."

"Fine," I said and hung up the phone. It rang again and I threw it against my bed. Then the tears started again. I went over to my computer to see who was logged on: there was Sam's name and I stared at it for a minute. He *had* to have seen that I was on and didn't try to chat with me, so no way would I ever say hi to him now.

"Emmi, come down for dinner," my mother shouted from downstairs.

"I'm not hungry."

"I don't care if you're hungry. Get down here—now."

"Go to hell," I replied.

"Watch your mouth, young lady. I don't know what happened last night, but I am *not* going to let you take it out on us. Come down here and sit at the table with us." With that one, I knew my mom meant business, so I trudged down the stairs.

I walked into the kitchen to find my whole family around the table. Between all of our sports schedules and my dad always working late, that was a rare sight.

"Nice hair," Eli said, laughing.

"Screw you."

"Emmi, stop it. Listen, you can tell us what's bothering you or not," my mother said.

"Not."

"Fine," my mother said. "Have some dinner." Jeremy passed me the chicken.

"I don't eat meat, dork," I said to him.

"No duh. Pass it to Dad." I gave the chicken to my father. I put a little salad on my plate; my mom makes great salad, but tonight I just wasn't in the mood. I poured on some balsamic vinegar and poked at it.

"So, Emmi, how was your day?" my father asked. Boy, where had he been?

"Her day sucked, Dad," Jeremy answered for me.

"Why?"

"That's the big mystery," Jeremy said.

"I broke up with Sam." Then I shoved my chair away from the table and hurried back upstairs, breathing heavily by the time I reached the top of the stairs. I hated my life. Maybe it'd be easier if I could just die.

27

Back in my room, I flopped down on my bed. I didn't think I had any more tears, but evidently there were still a few left. My nose was running again and I found a tissue, then heard someone at my door and looked up—my mother. Boy, she just didn't give up. I didn't even have the energy to tell her to leave, so she came in and sat on my bed.

"I'm sorry, honey," she said.

"It was the one good thing I had—and I blew it," I said between sobs.

"I know how hard this is for you," she said.

"No. You don't. You don't know what it's like to sit home all day because you don't have the strength to make it through a school day. And I miss school—I never thought I'd say that, but I do. And then I get together with this great guy, and even with everything that's going on, he's been so totally there for me, and then I go and blow the whole thing over some stupid pact."

Oh, God. Am I telling her too much? This was my mother; we didn't usually talk like this.

"What pact? What are you talking about?"

"You wouldn't understand." My mother married her first boyfriend—Dad. They were together since they were seventeen—that's like forever.

"I might, you know."

"Mom, it's about sex. And I don't think I can talk to you about this."

"You didn't have sex with him, did you? Your heart ..." She sounded panicky—exactly the reason I didn't want to have this conversation.

"It had nothing to do with my heart. And no—I didn't have sex with him."

Her whole body relaxed. "Is that why you broke up?" she asked.

I nodded.

"Then maybe it wasn't meant to be."

"Don't give me that. It was a great relationship. We clicked in so many ways. We just stumbled over something stupid—except he didn't think it was stupid. I so hate guys."

"I think the expression is 'Sometimes they think with their little heads instead of their big ones,'" she said.

"Mom!" *Did she really just say that—to me?*

"Pretend I didn't just say that. But you understand what I'm telling you, Emmi. It sounds to me like you did all the right things. And I'm sorry it didn't work out—I like Sam."

"Yeah, me too."

"You never know—he might come back."

"But you didn't see his face when he left," I said, thinking about how Sam didn't even look at me as he got into his car. "And I feel really guilty—I was totally bitchy to Becca."

"Why? What did she do?"

"Long story, but I probably should call her and apologize."

"Okay. I'll go downstairs and give you some privacy," she said.

"Thanks, Mom. I love you."

"I love you, too, Em." She walked out of my room and closed the door.

Becca didn't answer her cell, which didn't surprise me. I went to the computer and saw that she was online.

Emmi: *Bec, u there?*

I waited a bit and she didn't answer. But she hadn't signed off, so I figured she was just ignoring me.

Emmi: *Bec, I'm sorry. I was an idiot.*
I waited.
Emmi: *Sorry, sorry, sorry. Please say something.*
Becca: *It's not my fault your boyfriend is an asshole.*
Emmi: *I know.*
Emmi: *He's not an asshole. He's just . . . a guy.*
Becca: *Have u heard from him?*
Emmi: *No.*
Becca: *How r u?*
Emmi: *Out of Kleenex.*
Becca: *Stay strong, girl.*
Emmi: *EZ for u 2 say. Hey, did u have a game 2day?*

Becca: *Yeah, we lost 2 Nyack. Again. U better get better soon. We need our star forward.*

Emmi: *I miss it. I'm getting fat. And my muscles are totally gone.*

Becca: *I bet it'll happen soon. You have 2 keep hangin' in.*

Emmi: *Yeah. Thanks. Gtg. Talk tomorrow.*

Becca: *bi bi.*

I fell asleep around nine-thirty but I was up again at two. I tried everything I could think of to fall back to sleep. I even got *The Crucible* out again, but nothing was working. The last time I looked at the clock by my bed, it was four forty-five a.m. Next thing I knew, Eli was in my room and light was streaming through my blinds.

"Emmi, Emmi—wake up. You've got company," he said, jumping on my bed. He was wearing the soccer jersey I brought him back from Italy last summer; he had a brown smudge above his lips, so he must have had his favorite breakfast: Eggo waffles with melted chocolate chips.

"What time is it?" I asked, struggling to open my eyes.

"Seven," he said.

"I don't have to go to school, remember? Go away and let me sleep."

"Emmi, somebody's here to see you."

"Who?"

"Sam."

"Are you kidding?"

"Why would I make that up?" I looked out the window next to my bed and saw Sam's car in front of my house.

"Tell him to give me a minute," I said. I looked in the mirror and it was worse than I thought. My hair was totally messed up, and it was too far gone for a brush to fix. I grabbed the pink Yankees hat Jeremy bought me for my fourteenth birthday and put it on my head, threw on a pair of sweats under my nightshirt, and dabbed a little blush on my cheeks. I needed more time, but Sam had to be at school soon. So despite my better judgment, I headed down the stairs.

My mom was in the kitchen having breakfast with Jeremy. Puzzled at not seeing Sam, I looked questioningly at Eli, who opened the front door. There was Sam, sitting on the step and holding a wilting bunch of purple tulips.

"Hi," I said, not sure how to greet him. I pointed to my hat. "Sorry I'm a little . . ."

He stood up and came over to me. "These are for you," he said, handing me the lopsided bouquet. "I know you love purple—I picked them from my mom's garden. There aren't any flower shops open this early. I know they're a little sad, but it's the thought that counts, right?"

I stared at him, thrilled he was there, but not sure what was coming next.

"I didn't sleep much the past two nights," he confessed.

"Yeah, me either."

"I was such an idiot. I'm sorry." He lowered his voice to a whisper. "The sex shouldn't matter to me, but it did. But the more I thought about it, the more I realized how much I like you, and how the things I like about you are way more than the physical stuff—not that I'm not attracted to you because I am—you're beautiful. You've got a great body, and a fabulous smile." He traced my dimple with his finger. "And I love your hair."

"Now I know you're lying," I said, touching my baseball cap.

"No—I like your hair. I don't want some straight-haired carbon copy of every other girl. I want you." I smiled, but I couldn't meet his eyes. "We talk—really talk. The guys I hang with aren't smart. And they don't think it's cool to study or care about school. But I want to do well and go to a great college, and someday have an interesting job. They just want to talk about the baseball team or how hot some girl is, and things like that. Which is fine sometimes, but I like what we have, too. I don't want to lose it over sex." He took his hand and lifted my chin. Our eyes met and locked.

"And here I was, all set to sleep with you," I said.

"Really?" he asked.

"No." I laughed, and he smiled.

"Let's just have fun and get you better. After that, we'll go from there."

I gave him a small kiss on the lips, making my agreement clear. Then I heard giggling and turned around to see Jeremy and Eli peeking out the window. We'd been speaking quietly, but I didn't know how much they heard.

But I didn't care. Sam was back!

28

Dear Mom and Dad,

Since I basically sit home all day doing nothing but waiting for some other kid to die, I thought I'd take the time to write everyone letters, in case something happens to me and I don't make it.

I know I haven't been that much fun to be around lately. You always read stories in the newspaper about kids who're sick and totally cheerful, and who make everyone laugh. That hasn't exactly been me and I'm sorry for that.

We've been waiting for a heart for 4 months. I thought I was impatient in April, but now it's June and I'm out of my mind. I know it can't be easy for you guys to try to go about your regular life and still take care of me (along with Jeremy and Eli). I don't say it enough, but I love you guys and I really do appreciate everything you're doing for me. I know I can be snotty sometimes and not the nicest daughter, and I'm sorry. I wish I could have been better.

So thanks for being great parents and for always being supportive of all of my soccer playing (Dad) and for help-

*ing me with my schoolwork (Mom) and for driving me
EVERYWHERE, and generally putting up with me.*

You're the best.

Love,

Emmi

Dear Becca,

My BFF, my soccer bud, my travel companion . . .

*No matter what happens to me you better keep playing
soccer. And kiss a few guys for me. What the heck, kiss a lot
of guys for me! And make sure Sam mourns for a while, but
not too long—he's only 17.*

*I couldn't have gotten through everything these past
few months without your constant connection to school and
your cheerleading. You're my lifeline. You stuck by me
when you didn't have to, and I love you for it.*

Love ya!

Emmi

Dear Jeremy and Eli,

*If you're reading this that means I'm dead. And I guess
it means that one of you will get my room. I would like you
to keep the purple wall color to remind you of me, okay?
(How can you deny your dead sister anything, right?) Oh,
never mind, paint it whatever color you want.*

*You guys are great, even if you were usually pests. Eli,
I wish I could watch you play soccer in high school and in
college. I think you might be good enough to go pro and I
would've enjoyed seeing that. Jeremy, you baseball rebel,*

keep up the good work and don't forget to study—you need something to fall back on in case you don't make the Majors. You're pretty smart—maybe you could be a doctor and try to solve heart disease or do some other good things in my memory. No pressure, though!

Take care of Mom and Dad—they're going to be very sad. Be sad for a little while, too, but not for too long. Oh, and could you each name a baby after me when you grow up? I like Ella for a girl and Ethan for a boy. Or you could use Emmi as a middle name for a girl, too. Either way works.

Your big sister forever,
Emmi

I couldn't write one to Sam. I know I should, because he should have something of mine if I died. But I couldn't put it all into words. Maybe I'd just give him a copy of *Romeo and Juliet* or something.

29

Occasionally the jailers let me out, and one Saturday morning I wanted to go to the high school to watch Sam play baseball.

"Be careful," my mom said as she dropped me off. "Call me if you want me to pick you up."

"I'll get a ride home with Sam," I told her. "And I'll be fine. Stop worrying."

"Why don't you tell me to stop breathing," she said and I smiled; I was grateful that she let me go out. We said goodbye, and then I walked slowly to the baseball field. In my town, high school baseball doesn't draw the same kind of crowds football and basketball might, but there were about thirty people in the stands—mostly parents from the look of it, and a few girls in miniskirts sitting on the bottom row of the bleachers, probably trying to get the attention of the hot guys on the team.

I took a deep breath, enjoying the smell of the freshly cut grass; sometimes a simple smell can make you happy, and the memories of newly mowed soccer fields filled my mind. But I tried not to think about that too much—I'd done a good job lately of blocking out thoughts of soccer, afraid that if I let myself miss it, I'd be too depressed to get out of bed.

I walked past the miniskirts and climbed up the rickety metal stands, taking a seat near the top. I felt people staring at my IV lines and the medicine pack, but I wasn't sure if I was just being paranoid. The sun was in my eyes and I regretted not bringing my sunglasses; it'd been so long since I spent much extended time outside, I forgot about needing them.

The scoreboard said it was the third inning and our team, the Rams, was down 5-3. They still had plenty of time to catch up, and Sam, playing first base, was so focused he didn't see me. It was fun cheering for him, though, and I felt like one of the players' girlfriends you see on the jumbotron at Yankee games, cheering for my guy and his team.

A few innings later, a girl I recognized as a senior came up the bleacher steps, her high heels pinging the metal as she climbed, and sat next to me. She was one of those super-prissy cheerleader types with her tiny nose and her tiny legs and her perfect straight hair that she liked to toss for emphasis. And she smelled like one of those overpowering perfume inserts in magazines—so much for my fresh air.

"Hi. You're Emmi, right?" she said. I wasn't sure if I was supposed to answer.

"Yeah. And you are?"

"Ashley." Why are they always Ashley or Tiffany or Brittany?

"I've heard you're Sam's latest fling," she said. How do you answer that one? I went with sarcasm.

"Well, I'm his Saturday girl, which is why I got to come to the game. The Sunday girl gets to go to church with him, and I wasn't into that."

"Yeah, that makes sense."

No it doesn't—I'm kidding. Is this the part where I'm supposed to act all paranoid, worried that he has a different girl at every game? But I wasn't biting.

"You're a lot prettier than his last two girlfriends," she continued.

What am I supposed to say now? "Um, thanks. Are you a big baseball fan or are you here to see one of the guys on the team?"

"I've been dating David, the captain, for three years. I thought *everyone* knew that."

"Wow, you're like, practically married." More sarcasm, but like everything else, it seemed to go over her head. They say stupid people have no capacity to understand sarcasm, and Ashley seemed to be living proof.

"It does feel like that sometimes," Ashley said with a pleased grin. She pointed at the tubes running up my arm. "What's that?" she asked.

"Just my medications. I'm waiting for a heart transplant—I thought *everyone* knew that."

"Oh, " was all she said. Now there's a great conversation ender, and I figured she'd leave—but she didn't.

We watched in silence together, and it was now two outs in the bottom of the final inning, and we were down

6-4. Our team was at bat, there was a man on second base, and the tying run was at the plate. A player with giant biceps swung hard, but went down on three pitches. Then Sam stepped up to the plate. The Tigers pitcher was throwing hard, but looking a little tired. Sam let one go by and the ump called it a ball. The next one was a perfect strike. Why didn't he swing? The stands grew silent; the next pitch came and I held my breath. It seemed like it was going to hit the outside corner of the plate and Sam swung. The loud crack told me he'd hit the ball and I let out my breath as Ashley grabbed my hand and stood up in excitement, pulling me up with her. The crowd was on its feet as Sam rounded first base and headed toward second; he'd hit the ball deep into center field, where the center fielder got it and hurled it to the second baseman, who tossed it to the shortstop on second just as Sam slid into the base. It felt like an eternity as the crowd waited for the field umpire to make the call.

"You're OUT!" he shouted and everyone in my section of the bleachers screamed in protest.

"What are you, blind?" one dad yelled. I watched as Sam walked off the field, dejected. This was not going to be good.

"That ump's such an idiot," Ashley said, then clattered down the bleachers to go see her David. I didn't know what I should do; I wanted to go say hello to Sam, but I wasn't sure what kind of mood he'd be in after losing the game. I needed to say something though—he was my ride home.

I carefully made my way down the bleachers and over

toward the dugout. Sam threw his equipment into his bag and the dust flew up as he kicked at the dirt.

"It was a good hit, Sam," his coach said to him. "These things happen."

"I shouldn't have run," Sam answered.

"I sent you," the coach said.

"I should have known not to go."

"Sam, the center fielder made an unbelievable play. It's okay."

"It's not okay, but thanks, Coach." He looked up and saw me there. I smiled at him and he just continued to pack his things.

"Sorry you lost," I said, but he didn't answer. "Did you see me up in the stands? I was there since the third inning."

"I didn't notice."

I had to get him out of this funk, so I leaned over and whispered in his ear, "I met David's girlfriend, Ashley. She thinks we're best friends now."

"That's nice," he said flatly. Nothing I said was getting through to him.

"Are you always this cheery after a game?"

"Only when it's my fault we lose," he snapped.

"I'm sorry, Sam. But listen, I think you want to be alone right now. I still need a ride home, but I'll take a walk while you go to the locker room and get changed. We can catch up after that." When he didn't say anything, I walked away. He was so angry that it outweighed his usual protectiveness because he let me go without a word.

I walked across the baseball field toward the tennis

courts where a few senior citizens were hitting a ball around. They were doing pretty well. I hope I'm still playing soccer when I'm that age; it was a funny mental picture of Becca and me running down the field together with our wrinkles and gray hair, hers still as perfect as ever.

Then I looked past the tennis court to the soccer field. There was a game going on, which was odd because it wasn't high school soccer season, unless—omigod—it was my travel team playing in the spring league. I had so successfully blocked out soccer that it didn't occur to me they might be playing at school today.

I didn't want to go over and watch, but it was like I had no control over my body. Before long I was standing on the sidelines watching my old team play. Becca was tough in goal; the other team made a shot and her long arms grabbed it in a diving catch. She stood up and flung the ball across the field, and our forward, Katie Thomas, got the ball and started dribbling toward their goal, but she was stopped almost immediately by the other team's defense. I would have gotten around their halfback—she didn't seem that good. With each play I calculated how I would have done it differently—and of course better.

"Pass!" I heard someone shout as Lauren got caught between two defensive players. Then I realized I was the one shouting. Several players on the bench turned toward me, one of whom was Katie, who'd been taken out after missing several opportunities to score. She came over and gave me a hug.

"Emmi, omigod! How are you?" she asked.

"I'm good, but you guys don't look so hot."

"Ouch—not nice."

"Sorry, but you could be doing a lot better. Do you see their fullback? She's kind of chubby and slow. You need to take the ball over to the goal on her side so you have a better chance of getting past her."

"If it's so easy, you do it."

"I wish I could. *God*, I wish I could." There was another shot on our goal; Becca knocked it down, but their forward followed it right up and kicked again, this time getting it into the corner of the net.

There was an extra uniform in a mesh bag beside the bench and I picked it up. Maybe I could put this on and go in for a few minutes, enough to score and get us back in the game. How bad could a little running be? I put the uniform over my head and went to put my arms in the sleeves. But I couldn't get them through with the lines running up my arm and the thought of my medicines slapped me back to reality. And Becca drove home that point.

"Are you out of your mind?" she shouted as she left the field for a time-out.

"Yeah, I think I was," I said, taking the shirt off. "But you guys so need me."

"You think you're so great you can come in and win the game for us, even now?"

"I kind of do."

"Well, you're great, but you're not playing this season, are you? So you're not much help."

I just turned and walked away. I couldn't take this on

top of Sam's sulking; now Becca had gotten all pissy on me, too. I was beginning to think I should have stayed home.

"Wait, Emmi. I'm sorry," Becca called after me.

"Go play the game," I shouted back in my most forgiving voice. I wanted her to focus on the game, not worry about me. "I'll talk to you later." What is it about sports that makes everyone so crazy?

This day was taking a lot out of me. I started walking to the parking lot when I saw Sam coming toward me. His hair was wet, so I figured he had showered. I was trying to gauge his mood by his walk, but I couldn't tell anything.

"Hi," he said. I still wasn't sure, but then he gave me the cutest, most apologetic look and shrug, and we started laughing. "I'm sorry," he said, finally.

"You should be. But I'm sorry you lost." He hugged me and I leaned into him, feeling really tired by now.

"Thanks for coming."

"You really didn't know I was there?"

"I had no idea. I get kind of focused when I'm playing."

"That's an understatement." We walked past the other cars. "I do think Ashley is my new BFF."

"Yeah, you guys have a lot in common," he said.

"Oh yeah, I'm hoping to get together with her and we can do our nails and talk all about how lucky we are to be dating hunky baseball players."

"You think I'm hunky?"

"Dreamy."

"Dreamy?"

"Scorchin'."

"I'm scorchin'?"

"Red hot."

"Wow. If only I'd been safe at second—then I'd really be hot."

I smacked his shoulder and we laughed as we headed to his car.

30

June in New York is a great time of year. It's not buggy yet, and it's nice enough to spend the whole day outside. I started doing my schoolwork at the table on our patio. I'd tried my best to keep up with my classes all this time, but sometimes it was very discouraging. I felt lousy and tired, and I wondered why I was bothering. But most of the time it kept me connected to my friends. Becca usually brought my work over and Sam and I studied together a lot. Lauren was in all of my classes, so we spent a lot of time on the phone going over the tougher assignments. I'd taken the SATs in May and had managed to do fairly well.

June was also prom time, and everyone I knew was obsessed with the Junior Prom: who was going with whom, what they were going to wear, what parties you were going to, and whose parents would let them go to one of the no-alcohol clubs in New York City or to the New Jersey shore afterward. I wasn't surprised when my parents freaked when I told them I wanted to go.

"There is no way you're going," Mom said to me.

"She's not going," she told my father late one night as they were watching TV up in their bedroom. I turned the TV off and stood in front of it, blocking their view.

"You are not listening to me," I said. "It's not fair."

"No, it's not fair. But we're worried about you, and a prom isn't a reason to risk everything."

"You let me go to the movies."

"That's different."

"How?"

"It just is. Tell her, Dan."

"We're trying to protect you, honey." Did he mean it, or was he just siding with my mother?

"Bullshit with the protecting," I shouted.

"Language, Emmi," my mother corrected.

"Bullshit with the language. *Bullshit, bullshit, bullshit.*"

"Emmi!"

"No—I'm sick of all this. I sit around all day, missing absolutely everything. All I want is this one night. I'm asking to be a normal person again—for just one night."

"I think it's too risky," Mom said.

"Risky in what way?" I asked.

"All that excitement."

"I'm not allowed to get excited anymore? Are you kidding me?" This was ridiculous.

"No, honey—it's just that—Dan?" My mom was clearly at a loss for giving me a rational explanation.

"We're afraid there'll be—you know—drinking and that kind of thing." Oh, so there was an explanation, but it was an irrelevant one.

"You're afraid I'll drink? Do you think I'm that stupid?"

They hesitated.

"Come on—after all this time, I've been so good, and that's what you're afraid of? You guys truly suck." And with that I walked out of the room. Parents can be such assholes sometimes.

But there was no way I was giving up; I had to be subtle and strategic, and I waited for my next appointment with Dr. Leavens to move forward with my plan.

"Hi, Emmi. How are you doing?" Dr. Leavens began her usual mantra.

"Same, I guess."

"Do you have any swelling? More shortness of breath?"

"I've been a little more tired lately, but when I take a nap I feel better."

"Anything on your mind that you want to talk about?" She stepped closer to me with the question.

"Well, yeah, there is. The Junior Prom's coming up and I'd like to go with my boyfriend. That sounds okay, right?"

"What?!" My mother leapt out of her seat. "We told you no."

"It wouldn't be too bad," I said. "Would it, Dr. Leavens?" *Please back me up*. "For one night I just want to be normal."

"You can't! Dr. Leavens, please tell her she can't do this," Mom sputtered. "She can go to the Senior Prom next year. There's no need to take a chance for this one."

"What if I'm not around next year?" I shot back. The adults had no answer to that.

Dr. Leavens looked from me to my mother and back to me again. I knew I shouldn't have put her in the middle like this, but it was my only chance.

"If you're careful, I don't think it would be a problem for you to go," she said. *Thank you, Dr. Leavens.*

"I was wondering if it was possible to disconnect my medicine pack for a few hours, so I don't have to wear it at the prom."

"Are you kidding me!" my mother shouted. I knew I'd pay for this later, but for now I just wanted Dr. Leavens to back me up.

"You probably could disconnect the medicines for a few hours," Dr. Leavens said. "But there could be extreme complications and I don't know any doctor who'd recommend that a patient do that—even for the prom. I'm sorry, Emmi, but I think you should try to figure out a way around it and keep it connected."

"Yeah, this fanny pack will look lovely with the black dress I had in mind."

My mother wasn't convinced yet. "Do you really think it'd be okay for her to go?" she asked Dr. Leavens. "Because it seems awfully risky to me."

"I think if she's reasonable and careful, she should be just fine," Dr. Leavens said. "Of course, there can be no drinking and no overexertion."

"I don't know," my mother said.

"I bet Aunt Mindy'll be there," I said, realizing it for

the first time. "That'd be good, right?" I pleaded with my mom.

My mother shrugged; she looked worried and uncertain, but also resigned. I'd won this battle—finally.

"Wait," said Dr. Leavens, "I have an idea about the meds. You're wearing black?"

"Well, I haven't exactly found a dress yet."

"Try to get something in black. I have a great bag you can borrow; it's black with tiny rhinestones and we could fit the pump into it. You might still see the lines, depending on what type of sleeves you have. But I could come over and help you set it up. I think it could actually work."

"You'd do that? You wouldn't mind?" Dr. Leavens shook her head no. "Mom, what do you think?"

"It's very nice of Dr. Leavens to do that for you."

I could hardly speak and grateful tears filled my eyes. All I could manage was a muffled "Thank you."

31

Now that I had a green light for the prom, Mom and I found a great black dress. But it wasn't easy. At first I wanted a long-sleeved dress to hide the IV lines, but that didn't turn out to be realistic in June. Besides, the sleeves would have looked lumpy with the lines in them, and that would have called as much attention as the lines themselves. That's why we picked a cute black dress cut in a V in the front and back. It wasn't too low cut—my mom wouldn't have allowed that (and my dad *really* wouldn't have gone along with it). Because the IV lines were clear and would come up my arm into Dr. Leavens's cute little shoulder bag, I'd be able to carry the meds all night and still have my hands free. And I could avoid wearing that stupid fanny pack—which would have really messed up my look.

I got my hair cut and blown out very straight on prom morning. The stylist put a ton of hairspray on and I was happy it was a clear day since even the tiniest bit of humidity would've frizzed it out the second I left the shop. Becca and I decided to get manicures—not something "soccer chicks" did often, but it was nice to splurge every once in a while and get pampered.

After all the beauty prep I went home and took a nap—my afternoon routine these days. How pathetic that even the simple act of having your nails and hair done tired you out to that degree. I lay down carefully, not wanting to mess up my hair too much, and I fell quickly into a deep sleep. Then, in what felt like only a few minutes, someone was calling my name.

"Emmi, wake up. It's time to get ready." My mom was standing next to my bed and Eli darted into the room.

"WAKE UP, EMMI!" Eli shouted. "Time to get bee-you-ti-ful!" I threw a pillow at him and missed. I still felt tired but knew I had to shake it off. Then I felt my hair, hoping it was still smooth.

"Is my haircut still on?" I asked, still a bit groggy. This was a family joke: when Eli was two, he was excited about his first haircut. Afterward, we were doing other errands, and he fell asleep in the car. When he woke up, he felt his head and this tiny voice piped up from the backseat with: "Is my haircut still on?" Ever since, whenever any of us got haircuts or special work done, we always asked for a hair-check in those words.

Mom reassured me: "You look fine, Emmi. We'll run a brush through it before you go. Why don't you start getting ready? Dr. Leavens will be here in about a half hour." Mom pulled me up into a sitting position, and then I got up and walked into the bathroom, where I looked at my reflection in the mirror. As usual since I got sick, I was pasty white. What happened to the girl who'd been outside all the time and always had a fabulous tan by mid-June? But I knew it was easy enough to fix with a little makeup and blush.

I came downstairs dressed and made up a half hour later; my face was brighter and Mom had helped me into my dress. My medicine pump was still in the fanny pack, but that'd be taken care of soon. Then the doorbell rang and Eli opened the door. I almost didn't recognize Dr. Leavens in her jeans and a ponytail. Even with her high-heeled boots she was still tiny. And as promised, she brought the cutest little black bag with rhinestones on the edges.

"How're you doing?" she asked, my doctor first and foremost. I guess you can take the doctor out of the office, but you can't take the office out of the doctor.

"I'm good, thanks. A little tired, but excited about tonight."

"You look beautiful, and I love your hair straight and smooth like that." She examined my IV lines and said, "Now, let's see if we can work this out," and took the medicine pump out of its case. She looped the black bag's strap over my shoulder and slipped the pump inside it. But now, with the bag hanging from my shoulder, the lines that usually went up my arm and all the way down to the fanny pack were much too long.

"I don't want to replace these lines and don't have shorter ones with me anyway. Let's see if there's a way to arrange them in the bag without crimping them, because if they bend, you won't get your meds. Think of it like a bent garden hose that you can't use to water your garden." She tried to loop the IV lines around the pump, but for some reason they kept coming loose.

"This isn't going to work!" I said, getting frantic. Sam'd be here in fifteen minutes and we were running out of time.

"I'm not ready to give up yet," Dr. Leavens said. "Let me think for a minute." She quietly studied the pump, but I'm not good at silent. Then Eli came to see what we were doing; the last thing I wanted right now was a wise crack from him.

"Hey, why don't you wind the tubes around the inside of the bag and tape them there?" he said. "That way they won't close up or pop out." Amazing—the nine-year-old pest had solved my IV problem!

I lowered the bag slightly from shoulder height and Dr. Leavens climbed on a chair so she could see into the bag. Eli, the future engineer, cut pieces of medical tape and handed them to Dr. Leavens, who taped the lines that were wound against the lining of the bag. One of them popped up, but Dr. Leavens used four more pieces of tape to get them to stick.

When she got off the chair, Dr. Leavens gave me a careful and uncharacteristic hug, then said, "You look beautiful, Emmi; have a great time tonight. Keep an eye on the pump, but don't get too obsessed with it—we've taped it pretty tight. And I have my beeper on, so page me if you have any problem." She hugged me once more, said goodbye to my mom, and left.

My mom set my cell phone on vibrate and put it in the bag; there was no way I'd ever hear it at the prom. She even tossed in my hospital beeper, just in case.

"It probably won't happen tonight, but you never know," she said.

Ten minutes later the doorbell rang; Eli opened the door and went to jump on Sam, who put his hands up in the air to stop him.

"Don't mess up the tux, dude," he said, high-fiving Eli instead.

Sam looked so handsome in the simple tuxedo and black bowtie. His shoulders looked broader than usual, and I loved how his pants were cut so that his backside . . . well, in a word, he was *hot*.

"You look great," Sam said, his smile lighting up his whole face. Then he took me in his arms for a big hug.

"Careful of my bag," I warned.

"Got it—hey, your hair's straight."

"I know, now it's just like everyone else. But I wanted to try it."

"You look good this way, but I still like it curly, too. Come here." He opened the front door and pulled me outside to see a white limousine waiting for us. "How do you like that?" he asked.

"Wow."

"We'll pick up Becca and Eric at Becca's." Eric was one of Sam's friends from the baseball team and Sam thought Becca would have fun with him at the prom. "He's no rocket scientist, but he's a good guy," was his exact recommendation. But other than that, he was pretty hot looking and Becca figured he'd look good in the prom pictures. It wasn't going to be a night for deep conversation anyway. "And that way if you get tired, you can go outside and sit in it for a little while to get away from everything." Sam looked at my mom when he said this. She smiled at him and nodded.

"Sounds great," I said. And my mom agreed.

"You thought of everything, Sam. Thank you," she said.

"I try," he said.

After my mother took too many pictures, posing us by the flowering tree, by the front door, next to the limo, and every other place she could think of, Sam finally opened the limo door for me and we got in. Just as we were pulling out, my father and Jeremy drove up; they made us get out of the limo so they could inspect our outfits. Jeremy's baseball uniform was covered in dirt so I stayed far away but gave him a little wave. I hugged my dad and we got back into the limo. I waved to them all as we drove down the street, and I wasn't sure but thought there were some tears on my mother's cheeks.

32

Sam and I walked into the gym with Becca and Eric. The prom committee had done an awesome job of transforming the gym, and if not for the basketball hoops at either end, you'd never know you were in the gym. The prom's theme was "Life's a Beach," and there was a giant mural on one wall that showed waves on a beach. The decorating committee even set up a sand pit in front of the mural where you could have your pictures taken. And the DJ was on a wood plank stand made to look like a boardwalk. The tablecloths were sea blue, with some seashells scattered in the middle of each table. The lighting was dim, but in one corner there were colored lights giving a sunset effect. It was hard to believe this was still our gym with this total transformation, and I was so happy to be there. In a far corner, I spotted Aunt Mindy, who waved to me but didn't come over.

"Wow, some of these kids look pretty drunk," I said to Becca, who looked beautiful in her shimmering blue dress that matched her eyes. And *her* hair was, of course, perfect.

"Looks like we're the only ones who didn't go to an alcohol-fueled prepary," Becca commented.

"Those girls over there are probably wasted," I said, gesturing to a group of girls giggling uncontrollably in a corner.

"Look at how stupid John Starke looks dancing," she said, pointing at a guy with his tie off who was thrashing on the dance floor like some escaped lunatic.

"Emmi!" someone called out and I turned around to see a girl named Leanna who I knew from a few classes. She stumbled over and gave me a big drunken hug. "How're you?" she said, and before I could answer, she touched my lines and said, "God, I didn't think you'd be here, what with you being soooo sick. Like, how do you stand it? But you don't look as bad as people are saying." She slurred her words and I was trying to figure out how to get away from her so I looked at Becca.

"Omigod—isn't that Liam Reilly?" Becca said to Leanna, pointing to a guy across the gym as she tried to redirect her attention from me.

I picked up on it, saying, "Yeah, Leanna—I heard he's totally hot for you. Don't you want to go over and say hi?"

"Really, is he? I'm here with Lawrence, but we're just friends and"—she added in a drunken whisper—"I think he's gay."

"Well then, go over and talk to Liam—at least to say hi," I encouraged as I pointed her toward him with a little push. Leanna stumbled again and caught herself, then made a crooked beeline for poor Liam.

Becca and I laughed, looked at each other, and at the same time said, "Bitch."

"Let's go find the girls," she said.

"I'm dying to see their dates," I confessed. Lauren and Noelle didn't have dates till a week ago, when they went to South Village High—our rival school. They sat watching baseball practice, scoping out the guys, and when practice was over, they followed the team back to the locker room so they could get a closer view. Then, on their way out of the school, Lauren struck up a conversation with one of the players. One thing led to another, and by the time they left, both of them had dates for the prom. It turned out that Sam knew them from Little League and Eric knew one guy from church, so they weren't total strangers to us.

We took our guys and found Lauren and Noelle and their dates—each as smokin' as they'd bragged—and put our stuff at their table. The girls hung their evening bags on the backs of their chairs, but I could only take off my sheer wrap to save my seat; my bag wasn't going anywhere but my shoulder. I gave it a quick check to make sure everything was okay inside.

As a slow dance started, I took Sam's hand and led him to the dance floor.

"Are you okay doing this?" he asked.

"I think I can handle the slow ones."

We started dancing and I rested my arms on Sam's shoulders and he carefully put his arms around my waist, making sure to avoid knocking my bag around.

"Sorry about this bag," I said.

"Nah, don't worry about it."

"No, I—I can't believe how good you've been to me. I know this isn't easy."

Then he leaned down and kissed me—a really good, deep kiss. We continued dancing while we kissed for a while, and it was like the whole room disappeared and it was just the two of us.

"Get a room!" Eric called out as he and Becca danced past us and I floated back to reality, hearing Becca's happy laugh. Lauren was already hot and heavy on the dance floor with her date, Chris—that girl wastes no time warming up to a guy.

When the next song started, an upbeat dance tune I loved, I started dancing to it.

"Maybe we should sit down," Sam suggested, concerned I was overdoing it.

"No—it's my prom and I *love* this song!" I grabbed his hand and we danced, even though the bag made it a little awkward. Sam was a great dancer, and we were going crazy on the floor; soon a group formed a circle around us to watch.

"Go, Emmi!" someone shouted and I danced even faster. It was exhilarating, and then Becca joined us in the middle of the circle, pulling along a reluctant Eric. But in a few more beats, even Eric got into it. The music was great and the crowd was clapping in time; it was awesome and we kept at it for three more songs.

Then the DJ announced dinner and put on mellow dinner music. Sam took my hand and I floated back to the table with him, and then we sat and started eating our shrimp cocktail appetizers.

Suddenly I was overwhelmed with exhaustion; Noelle was the first to notice.

"Emmi, what's wrong?" Noelle, my constant worrier, asked.

"I'm fine," I said, but I wasn't so sure. I was extremely tired—totally wiped out, in fact. And I'd started feeling kind of nauseated.

"Do you want to go to the limo for a little while and rest?" Sam asked.

"You're just tryin' to get lucky," Chris teased.

"She needs to rest," Sam snapped.

"I was kidding, man—chill out," Chris apologized.

"No, let's eat dinner," I said, not wanting to ruin anyone's night. But I sat there, barely able to eat, watching everyone chatter away as they ate, disconnected from them now, like I was just watching some reality television show. I couldn't join in with the conversation, and all I could do was sit there like a blob, poking at my mashed potatoes, but doing no more than move things around on the plate—my appetite was gone. When the dessert came it looked delicious—white chocolate mousse in chocolate cups drizzled with raspberry sauce; normally I'd have polished it off and fast, but I was too tired to care.

Becca, who was sitting next to me, leaned over, and said, "Em, why don't you go lie down for a while? Take a quick nap and then come back for the rest of the party," she said, standing up and grabbing my hand to pull me up. "Come on—don't argue with me."

I'd lost any ability to resist, and the thought of a nap sounded good. She walked me into the parking lot where we spotted our limo among many others—everyone's way of avoiding drinking and driving.

"Emmi's going to lie down for a while," Becca explained to the driver, who was talking to another chauffeur. He probably figured I was just another drunken prom girl about to puke in his limo; while I certainly wasn't drunk, puking was a definite possibility. Becca opened the door and we stepped into the limo, which had two couchlike seats facing each other. I lay down on one and she sat across from me.

"Go back in," I said. "You shouldn't miss the prom just because I'm a little tired."

"I don't mind."

"Bec, it's *prom*! I don't want you to miss any of it. Just come back and get me in a half hour, okay?" I said, my eyes closing involuntarily.

"I'll be back in a little while," she said.

"Don't do anything I wouldn't do," I said, drifting off to sleep.

I didn't know how long I'd been sleeping when Sam thrust the limo door open, got in, and kissed me on the cheek.

"Emmi, wake up."

"I'm sorry," I said, groggily.

"Emmi, you have to come back inside. You're not going to believe this—they voted us king and queen of the prom."

"What?" That totally woke me up.

"C'mon. We have to have our official dance."

"They voted *us* king and queen? Why?"

"Who cares? Let's just go. Are you okay, can you handle it?"

"I'm fine. But how's my hair?" I asked.

He smoothed it down, saying, "It looks great. C'mon—let's go." We climbed out of the limo and went back inside to our prom. When we got to our table, Becca, Lauren, and Noelle "group hugged" me, then Sam took my hand and we went up the steps onto the DJ's boardwalk, where we were given plastic crowns with fake jewels. I was so glad my hair was straight—it made the crown look better.

The DJ took the microphone and announced, "Ladies and gentlemen, may I present North Village High's king and queen of the Junior Prom: Emmi Miller and Sam Hunter."

I smiled at the crowd but couldn't see anyone with the lights shining in my eyes. All I was able to see was Becca, who'd snuck up front to take pictures with her cell phone. Sam took my hand and raised it in the air, and I waved to my court and blew kisses. Sam took a deep bow in my direction and I followed his royal lead, curtsying to him. Everyone applauded and I gave him a big hug. It was so totally awesome.

Sam led me onto the dance floor and everyone stepped aside; then, with the spotlight on us, the music started and we danced. I was still very tired, but Sam held me in his arms and it felt so good. He looked into my eyes and gave me one of his knockout smiles, and I rewarded him with a kiss, making the crowd cheer.

"Do you think they did this because they feel sorry for me?" I asked.

"Maybe they did it to show their support."

"I like your way of thinking better. Thanks—I'll take it." And then I kissed him again. We continued dancing together in the spotlight, but then, suddenly, I didn't feel so good.

"Stop spinning me," I said.

"I'm not spinning you, Emmi. We're just swaying."

"It feels like I'm spinning," I said, and I couldn't make that feeling stop. Sam stepped back a bit to look closely at my face, and then swept me off the dance floor as the crowd gasped in surprise. My legs began buckling and I begged, "Not here—not in front of everyone." I felt very lightheaded as Aunt Mindy ran to support me on the other side. When we got outside, I nearly collapsed, but Aunt Mindy and Sam caught me before I hit the pavement.

Everything was getting foggy and I found myself panting. Then I thought I heard someone say to call an ambulance, and someone else said I was ruining the prom—that hurt the most.

33

I woke up in the back of the limo, with Aunt Mindy and Sam on each side of me.

"Where . . . are . . . we . . . going?" It was hard to even get the words out—that's how wiped out I was.

"We're taking you to the hospital," Aunt Mindy said.

"I don't need the hospital. I'm fine. Can't we just go home?" I tried to sit up, but I was still way too woozy.

"You're not fine, Emmi, and you need medical attention right now."

"We're going there in the limo?"

"We decided it'd be faster than calling an ambulance, and besides an ambulance would have taken you to the local hospital instead of going to Children's."

I tried to sit up again and this time managed it. "See, I'm fine—really."

Sam took my hand. "Em, I hate to say it, but you look terrible. And your face turned gray when we were dancing—actually not even gray—you had no color at all. It was—well—kind of scary," Sam said.

"Gee, thanks."

I turned to Aunt Mindy and pleaded, "You can't tell my parents. They'll kill me," and started to cry. Aunt Mindy and Sam looked at each other.

"Sshh," she said. "I had to, honey. They're meeting us at the hospital."

Now I was totally screwed. "No! I'm fine. Let's just go back to the prom." I started pinching my cheeks to give them color, then said "Maybe it's just my meds." I checked my bag to make sure the pump was still working—it was.

But Aunt Mindy wasn't interested in my protests. "Emmi, you don't have a choice. Maybe it's nothing serious, but you have to see a doctor and let them determine if you're okay."

Who invited Aunt Mindy to this prom, anyway?

We got to the emergency room and climbed out of the car; they must not see a lot of limos pulling up to the ER entrance and people started gathering on the curb to see which celebrity was going to climb out. They must have been disappointed that it was a couple of high school kids in prom outfits with an English-teacher chaperone.

Aunt Mindy and Sam took their places on each side of me and that's how we walked into the emergency room. I'd never been to the ER on a Saturday night and it wasn't my idea of fun. We tried to find a seat, but they were all taken already. And what a scary bunch of patients these were: there was a guy in the corner holding a blood-soaked cloth against his arm; a toddler was screaming in his mother's arms; and a man on the sofa against the wall was moaning to himself and rocking. A pregnant lady screamed at a nurse in Spanish, and the place smelled like an awful combination of puke, disinfectant, urine, and baby food.

We finally found three seats and waited to be called. The tears started again, and Sam put his arm around me consolingly. I put my head on his shoulder and closed my eyes, dreading my parents' arrival—it wasn't going to be good. They'd told me not to go and I insisted; they were right, and I was almost more afraid of their reaction than I was of what was happening to my heart.

"Emmi!" I looked up and there was my mother, which only made my tears start up again.

"What happened? I knew this wasn't a good idea. I just knew it!" my mother said, standing over me.

"April, you said you weren't going to yell at her," my father said, taking her arm and pulling her back from me.

"I'm sorry, but I changed my mind," she said tensely.

"I'm sorry, Mom," I said, standing up. She took me in her arms and I started sobbing. "I'm okay now—really," I said between sobs.

"Emmi, you can't do these things right now. You have to take it easy until they find you a heart," she said. "You could've died."

"Did you sign in?" my father asked, trying to change the subject.

"They have all her information. Busy night here," Aunt Mindy answered.

"We called Dr. Leavens," my father told us. "She said she'd let the ER doctors know we're coming."

"If you two're all right, I'll take the limo back to the

prom," Aunt Mindy said. "I imagine your other friends might need it." I'd forgotten that Becca and Eric wouldn't have a way to get home, but someone would've taken them; this was Aunt Mindy's way of making a gracious exit. "Sam, do you want to come with me?"

Sam turned to my parents. "Is it all right if I stay here?" My parents looked at each other.

"It may be a while," my dad said.

"I don't mind. I wouldn't feel right going back to the dance without my prom queen," Sam said, taking my hand.

My parents looked at him, puzzled by that comment.

"They voted us king and queen of the prom," I explained.

"Before she turned gray and nearly collapsed. But she did get in at least part of her official dance," Sam added.

"I guess it was pretty unforgettable," I said.

"Yeah, they'll be talking about it for ages," Sam agreed.

"Great—just how I want to be remembered."

"I'm going to go check on how many people are ahead of you," my mother said. "But the gunshot wound and the screaming baby may take priority." Her sense of humor showed that her anger had subsided and she was back to her usual take-charge ways. Aunt Mindy walked her to the desk and hugged her goodbye; I couldn't hear the few words they exchanged before my aunt left.

Sitting in the waiting room, I fell asleep with my head on Sam's shoulder; it was an hour later when they finally called me. Sam nudged me awake, and Mom and Dad followed the nurse who'd called my name. People looked up as Sam and I walked by and I heard some whispers. One guy even whistled.

The four of us walked into a tiny exam room.

"Sam, maybe you and I should head back to the waiting room," my dad suggested.

Sam nodded and said, "I'll see you in a little bit."

I took off my dress and put on my favorite hospital gown. Someday I'm going to invent a better hospital gown, something stylish that covers you better. My mom had to help me hold my medicine bag while I stepped out of my dress and laid it carefully on the chair.

"It was a great prom," I told her. "I know you're mad at me, but it was worth it. It felt so good to be there."

"It was an unnecessary risk," she said.

"No, Mom, it was totally necessary. I'm sorry I ended up here, but I'm glad I went."

A doctor opened the door and came in—at least I thought she was the doctor, but she didn't look much older than me. She had a cute, short haircut and a funky blouse under her white coat.

"Hi, I'm Dr. Gerber," she said, shaking hands with my mother. "I'm one of the cardiology fellows here."

I guessed that was probably a notch up from a regular med student. Dr. Gerber proceeded to do the usual exam and took my history that by now I could recite in my sleep.

"Her blood pressure is a little low and her pulse is fast," she told us, talking directly to my mom; she was one of the doctors who barely looked my way, almost as if I weren't even there.

"What do you recommend, and have you talked to her doctor?" my mom asked.

"I spoke with Dr. Leavens," Dr. Gerber said, "and we'd like to admit Emmi overnight to keep an eye on her. We'll monitor her blood levels and medications, and then Dr. Leavens will see her in the morning."

The last thing I wanted was to spend my prom night in the hospital, but at this point I couldn't even protest. I had to let them do whatever they needed to do, and hope that with good behavior and a better heart rate I'd be out of there by tomorrow.

"You okay, Em?" my mother asked. I shrugged.

"Can I say goodnight to Sam before I go to the room?" I asked.

"We'll all go with you while you get settled," she answered.

"I want to get you a bed on the pediatric floor," Dr. Gerber explained. "It may take a little while, so please be patient."

"I've got nowhere else to be," I said, but I was wiped out and would've loved to go right to bed.

After the doctor left, Sam and my dad came back into the tiny room. We ended up waiting a very long time for my room, and it was just about daybreak by the time I finally got moved. It was crazy—if I was sick enough to be admitted, what sense did it make to keep me waiting in the ER all night? I really didn't get these hospitals.

I spent the next three days having my blood tested, my blood pressure checked, and my heart rate monitored. They thought I was having an arrhythmia—an irregular heartbeat—and wanted to watch me closely. I thought they should just give me one of those machines you can wear at home and let me go. It's called a Holter Monitor and I'd had them before. They put some stickers on your chest, attach wires to the stickers, and attach the whole thing to a machine that looks like a large iPod, which they put in a holder around your neck. It was annoying, but nothing like being stuck in the hospital.

I hated being there, even though I knew it was a great hospital. But I was constantly being checked and examined, sometimes by doctors surrounded by large groups of students. You lose your dignity and your privacy and I wondered why I had to be the focus of so much attention. I knew it was a teaching hospital, but did they have to teach my case to every student they had? That's what it felt like to me: I saw nurses, Dr. Leavens, fellows, residents, and medical students. There was always another person in a white coat introducing herself and examining me. Now that I was feeling better, all I wanted was to go home.

My parents were taking turns staying with me, and I told Sam and Becca not to bother visiting right now. They had to study for finals and besides, I wasn't really in the mood to entertain anyone anyway.

"Dad, are you disappointed with me?" I asked that second afternoon. I felt like every time he looked at me it was with sadness and disappointment.

"What are you talking about?" he asked, moving closer to my bed.

"This whole thing has kind of paused my soccer career. I know you were really into it."

"Emmi, are you kidding me? I just want to see you get better. Soccer means nothing to me compared to that."

"But I put in all those years and you paid all that money—and now I've blown it." I couldn't even look at him and started fiddling with my bed rail, pulling it up and down. Dad grabbed the rail and pulled my face to him.

"Okay, soccer may be important to us both; and yes, it's something you've worked for your whole life. But maybe this is just a speed bump that you'll get past and you'll go right back to training."

He understood how important this was to me. And I didn't have to let him down; I just had to get better soon and get on with it.

"I want you to—" He was interrupted by Dr. Leavens at the door.

"Hi, Emmi," she said. "How're you doing?" She proceeded to examine me.

"Will Emmi move up on the transplant list since she's hospitalized?" my father asked, as if his pushing could drive the whole thing forward.

"Not really. Thankfully, she's still not acute, and she's here more for observation than treatment. I think that if her levels stay fine and her rhythm's good, she'll go home tomorrow," she replied.

"And end up waiting some more," I said.

"Yes, Emmi—that's true and I'm sorry. But I'm very optimistic that a heart'll come soon."

"I'm bored out of my mind," I complained. "I thought I was bored at home, but this is way worse."

"I understand you have finals next week. It's impressive how you've kept up with your schoolwork," Dr. Leavens said.

"We're very proud of her," my father added.

"Woo-woo," I said, waving my finger sarcastically. "I just want to get on with it already."

"Emmi, I don't want to scare you, but you can't exert yourself like you did on prom night. No more dancing for a while," Dr. Leavens said. "You got lucky this time, but that kind of exertion could bring on a fatal episode next time."

Fatal, as in die? What the hell did I do? And how was I supposed to keep going, knowing I might have a fatal episode? *Fatal equals final. I could die.*

They finally let me go home the next day. Now I had to keep waiting and hoping it wouldn't be too much longer—and that I didn't do anything fatal.

34

"You got a letter from Becca," Jeremy said as Dad was taking him to his baseball game. "It's on the hallway table."

But I just ignored him.

"Don't you want to open it?" Dad asked.

"Not really," I said.

The letter wasn't suddenly going to make everything okay, so why bother? The only thing I wanted to hear was that there was a heart ready for me. I was so sick of waiting and worrying that something would happen before I could get a heart. Those weeks after the prom were long, boring, empty, and depressing—a real letdown after my one exciting night. While everyone else got to go on with their lives, here I was stuck at home waiting, with my entire life on hold—literally.

"Have fun," I mumbled as Jeremy grabbed his bat bag and opened the door, my father close behind. But I didn't mean it, not even a little. Why should he have fun when I couldn't?

"Emmi—," Dad started.

"I'm fine," I said, cutting him off. I just didn't want to hear it.

They finally left me, alone again with just my beeper and my meds. I sat on the couch holding the beeper in my hand, just staring at it and willing it to go off—telling me I had a heart.

If this beeper doesn't go off soon, I could die.
Die. Dead. Forever.

My mind tried to block it out, but it kept creeping back in.

Die. Dead. Forever.

What if something happens to me while I'm by myself? What if I'm on my way to the bathroom and my heart just stops? Dr. Leavens said that wouldn't happen, but how did she know? Was she lying so I wouldn't freak out? No one really knew how long my heart had left. Dr. Leavens kept telling me that if they were worried about sudden death—which they weren't—they'd admit me to the hospital again.

So maybe they weren't worried about sudden death, but I sure was. Before the prom I wasn't afraid to move around and tried to keep things normal. But now I thought maybe staying still might be a good thing; I couldn't just dance like crazy, or kick the ball around with my friends—or mess around with Sam—without serious consequences.

It totally sucked.

Nervously, I kept staring at the beeper, but it was silent. I checked the batteries to make sure they were working, then stared at it some more: nothing. I was sick of TV, sick of reading, and completely sick of sitting around waiting. Might as well take a look at Becca's letter.

Dear Emmi,

Greetings from Duke University in sunny North Carolina. And I mean sunny. What was I thinking going to soccer camp in North Carolina? It's HOT here. Speaking of hot, the Duke soccer players—Wow! We get to watch them train sometimes, and I've met a few of them. I know what you're thinking, and yes, they're good kissers. And no, I haven't slept with any of them (still waiting!).

I wish you were here—it's strange doing a soccer summer without you. The coaches here are cool and I'm working HARD. The dorms have no A/C—they're these beautiful gothic buildings, but who cares about that when they have no A/C?! It's breakfast/soccer/lunch/soccer/dinner/more soccer. Then we fall into bed exhausted. Yes, and alone. Get your mind out of the gutter.

Lauren and Noelle say hi. Lauren's driving me crazy— you're a much better roommate. Well, hopefully we'll all do something soccer-y together next summer. Actually, we'll be heading off for college next summer—Wow!

Hope you're feeling good. Hang in there. Kisses to Sam (as if I had to give you an excuse to kiss him!).

Love ya, Bec

Who cared about the stupid gothic buildings or the stupid soccer bodies? I tore the letter into a zillion little pieces and ran to the family room window and threw them outside.

Running to the window tired me out—my heart was pounding. I collapsed to the couch and tried to calm my heart back to its steady beat, breathing in and out and resting my head on the cushions. One little five-foot sprint and I was ready to take a nap.

Thank goodness school was over so I had no homework hanging over my head. I didn't know how I got through the spring semester, but somehow I'd managed to get As in all my classes, even though I was out since December. There's no way I could focus like that anymore now—I was way too tired. The couch was so comfortable. My heartbeat was slowing and I closed my eyes and nestled further into the cushions.

Then Mom came home and saw me lying there.

"Emmi, you okay?" she asked, shaking me awake. "We need to go."

The thought of getting off the couch exhausted me even more.

"Where?"

"Your doctor's appointment," she said. "Come on, we'll be late."

I'd forgotten all about my appointment with Dr. Leavens. What was the point, anyway? It was the same every time. She always said the same thing: "How are you feeling? Keep taking the meds. Blah blah blah."

"Do I have to go?" I asked, knowing the answer. Mom shot me one of her "give me a break" looks, then I slipped into my flip-flops and dragged myself out the door.

Mom and I got in her minivan and headed toward the city and she tried to fill the time with chatter, as usual.

"Sam coming over later?" Mom asked.

"Maybe," I said.

"How does he like being a camp counselor?" she asked.

"Fine," I said.

"What did Becca say in her letter? Does she like Duke?"

"Yeah." She was trying; I just wasn't up for playing along. But Mom got it—she turned on the radio and we rode the rest of the way without talking.

Once we arrived, parked, and headed for the doctor's office, my caffeinated mother was not used to walking at my heart-impaired pace. She kept zipping ahead, realizing I was behind her, and waiting for me to catch up.

"Sorry," she said, "I'm used to walking faster."

I shrugged. "I'm going as fast as I can go," I said.

"No—I know that. I do." She put her arm around me and gave me a little squeeze. Then, when we walked into the waiting room, through the sea of toddlers and their parents, I noticed Abe. And, for the first time all day, I smiled.

There was something so comforting about seeing him there, wearing a CROSBY, STILLS, NASH AND YOUNG tank top with his scar peeking out. He was obviously into old rock groups—my dad would love it.

Spotting me, he came right over. "Hi. I remember you," he said. "You were getting the transplant that day. How are you feeling? Are you here for a biopsy?"

"It didn't happen," I answered.

"You're kidding! Wow, that sucks. Are you still waiting?"

I nodded.

"Isn't it sick, hoping for someone to die?"

I nodded again and he sat down next to me. He wasn't supercute or anything, but there was something about him that had me totally intrigued. I couldn't put my finger on it; maybe it was his upbeat energy or the way he seemed totally comfortable with himself.

"Sometimes I feel guilty that I got some other kid's heart. But then I realize he was already dead and there was nothing anyone could've done to change that. This way, at least a little part of him stays alive," he said.

"That's a good way of looking at it," I said, smiling at him. I might have even thrown a dimple his way—I just wanted him to keep talking. What was it about this guy? He didn't even realize it, but he was pulling me out of my funk.

"I'm here for my biopsy," he said. "They go in and snip out a piece of your heart and test it for rejection." I grimaced at the thought. "I'm down to every few months now. And so far, no rejection."

"I have another checkup," I told him. "How long'd you wait for your heart?"

"Only a couple of weeks, but I was really sick. I was at the top of the list and they had me in the hospital. I would've died in a couple of days if I didn't get the heart."

"I'm home with a medicine pump, but I don't have enough energy to do much anymore."

"I hope it'll happen soon," he said.

"It feels like it'll never happen."

171

"It will, and you can have a beautiful scar like mine."
Abe lifted his shirt and flashed me his scar again.

"Any excuse to flash me, huh?"

"I've been working out. Someone has to appreciate it."

"Glad I could be of service." I shot another dimple smile his way.

"Emmi Miller," the nurse called.

"I better go." I wanted to sit there and listen to Abe for a little while longer, but I got up and started down the hall with my mother. Then Abe caught up with me and handed me a slip of paper with his e-mail address and phone number.

"Really—call me this time. E-mail, text, whatever. I'm around," he said. I shoved it in the pocket of my shorts.

"Thanks, Abe," I said. Our eyes met and we smiled at each other. Maybe that's what it was about him—he understood what I was going through—something nobody else could. He walked me right to the exam room.

"You can't come in," I told him.

"I thought maybe I'd listen in and reminisce about the time before my transplant."

"The good old days?"

"Nah, it's much better now. See ya later, Emmi."

Then he turned and walked back to the waiting room and I figured out what it was that intrigued me about him: he was alive. Not just heart-beating, still-walking alive, but happiness-bursting-from-every-cell-in-his-body alive.

Abe was a glimpse into the other side of this awful journey.

If I ever get the chance to reach the other side.

35

You know your life is pathetic when the big excitement of the day is getting *Cosmo Girl* in the mail. Everyone else was busy going on with their lives.

Becca and the girls were still away at Duke; Sam was playing camp counselor to a bratty group of six-year-olds at a local day camp and he came over at night if he wasn't too tired. My father was working night and day to land some new client, and my brothers were off playing sports most of the time. My mom only had to work mornings in the summer, so that gave us every afternoon together. After the first jigsaw puzzle was finished and we had done each other's nails, we ran out of buddy things to do.

"We were going to do college tours this summer," I reminded her one afternoon as we sat outside on the patio.

"You're right. I'd forgotten about that." She took a sip of iced coffee.

"I guess that's out for now." Hard to plan for next year when I didn't even know what tomorrow would bring—if there even was one.

"Well, just for now. Have you thought about where you might like to go?" she asked.

"I have to see who recruits me." Mom looked at me, puzzled.

I could pretend I wasn't worried, that my biggest concern was getting back to soccer, instead of whether I was going to die between now and soccer season. If I focused on soccer, maybe it'd get me past the fear. Dad understood this, but Mom didn't get it.

"Emmi, I'm not sure you'll be ready to play soccer this fall."

"But I have to! I have to get the heart and get myself back in shape as quickly as possible."

"Honey, it might not be that simple."

"Mom, it's the one thing driving me—a heart will come soon. And after I get it, I'll be the best rehab patient they've ever seen. I'm nothing without soccer, and I need to get back to it." I just needed that heart—and soon.

"That's not true at all. You're smart, you're great with kids. I thought you said you wanted to teach kids in Mongolia or somewhere like that."

"*After* the soccer. I've worked all these years for this. I'm not ready to give it up. Please don't take that away from me."

I could tell she didn't agree, but she realized she couldn't argue with me. If I didn't have this goal, this focus, I'd totally lose it. I picked up the book I'd been reading and read half a page before I realized I wasn't in the mood.

I left the patio and my mom, went inside, and turned

on the television, flipping through all the channels before I realized I wasn't in the mood for TV, either. The truth was, I wasn't in the mood for anything I was still allowed to do. But then I remembered something that *did* interest me.

Rifling through my dirty laundry pile, I found what I was looking for—the crumpled piece of paper with Abe's phone number, still in the pocket of my jean shorts. I grabbed my cell and dialed the number.

"Hello?" Abe answered.

"How'd you get through it?" I blurted. "Hello" would have been more appropriate, but I needed to know.

"Who is this?" he asked.

"Emmi—from the hospital. I'm not sure if you remember me, but—"

"Hi, Emmi! Sure, I remember you," he said. And I heard the smile in his voice.

"So how did you get through it?" I asked him again. "Here I am, waiting for something that'll save my life, and I'm ready to kill myself from the boredom." *And I'm scared a heart will never come, or it will come and something awful will happen despite it.*

"I didn't have to wait as long as you, but I guess I kept myself busy listening to music and thinking."

"I'm out of things to think about—I've thought through everything possible."

"I hate to say this, because I don't know you well, but you have to get over feeling sorry for yourself."

"How do you know I'm feeling sorry for myself?"

"Because I was there two years ago," he said. "So I know."

I flopped down on my bed and stared at the ceiling, trying to absorb what he was telling me. Was I feeling sorry for myself, truly? But didn't I have every right to feel that way? Who was he, telling me to get over it?

"You there?" he asked.

"Yeah," I said. "I'm just thinking about what you said. But I thought you were going to tell me the secret to keeping myself busy and making my days more interesting."

"I'm home doing nothing all day this summer," he said. "So maybe you could give me some advice instead."

"Get out of the house," I said. "Go for a run. Get a job. Hang with your friends. God—you can do anything—wish I were so lucky."

"Great idea. Except I'm a lousy athlete, and I have no skills and no friends."

"And no confidence, I see."

"Oh, tons of confidence," he said. "I'm confident I'm a lousy athlete and have no skills and no friends."

I laughed. "It's great talking to you, Abe," I said. "I may be sick as a dog, but at least I know I have great athletic ability, lots of skills, and tons of friends."

"Sure," he said. "Make me feel like crap."

"I don't know you that well, but maybe you need to stop feeling sorry for yourself," I said.

"Ouch. Okay, truce."

I heard my mother call from downstairs, saying lunch was ready. "I gotta go," I said. "Time for lunch."

"Call me again tomorrow," he said, "so my self-esteem can get another boost."

"By tomorrow, I'll expect you to have found a job and at least one friend."

"Does it count if I buy coffee for the homeless guy on my corner and hang with him for a while?"

"If he's willing to talk to you, it counts."

I was still laughing when we hung up.

36

After that, Abe and I talked every morning. We didn't get into anything superdeep; we mostly just kept each other company.

A few days later it was July Fourth. Each summer, my family took a big trip to the beach, renting a house for a week on Long Beach Island, off the New Jersey Shore. Each day we'd sleep late, eat a quick breakfast, and stumble out to the beach where we'd stay until the sun set. Then we'd get cleaned up and find some overcrowded place for dinner—something that came with French fries.

On the Fourth we would go out to the beach, set up a blanket, and watch the fireworks. My mom and dad would reminisce about all the other Fourth of Julys, and my brothers would fight over something stupid, like who had more room on the blanket. As I got older, it was embarrassing and I resented not hanging out with my friends.

This time I would've loved to be sitting on the beach with my family. But we didn't go anywhere that year—my parents were afraid to be too far from the hospital, just in case. We'd spent too many months doing things "just in case," and it was getting old.

Sam and I'd been invited to a barbeque one of the other camp counselors was having, but I didn't feel up to it. We decided he'd come over and we'd hang out.

"How do you want your steak?" my dad called to Sam from the grill in our backyard.

"Medium rare is fine," Sam answered.

"Emmi, bring me the pepper," my dad requested as he prepared my tuna steak. Since I had to be careful about my salt intake, he seasoned the fish with pepper instead of our usual soy-sauce-and-maple-syrup marinade.

After dinner, we stayed outside. Sam and Jeremy threw the baseball around while my parents, Eli, and I played Scrabble. Every once in a while Sam would look over my shoulder and suggest a word.

"Why don't you sit down and play?" I asked, after he'd done it the fourth time.

"No, I'd rather coach you," he said, throwing a high fly to Jeremy.

"Do you remember the year it was raining on the Fourth of July and Jeremy insisted on staying on the beach anyway, just in case it stopped raining and they started the fireworks?" my mother asked. Uh-oh—even without the beach, their reminiscing was starting.

"Or the year Emmi came down to the beach with two washcloths to hold over her ears so she wouldn't hear the noise from the fireworks?" my father added, laughing.

We heard the rumble from distant fireworks but

couldn't see anything. "I have an idea," my dad said, getting up from the table and going into the garage. He came out carrying our ladder and set it against the house. Was he going to clean the gutters to celebrate? Then he climbed up and walked onto the roof.

"Dan, you're crazy!" my mother yelled. "What are you doing up there?"

"I can see them," he said as another firework went off. "Come on up." The boys didn't hesitate—Jeremy and Eli scrambled up to the roof and sat beside my father. I looked at Sam, who shrugged his shoulders and walked with me to the ladder, which wobbled briefly, but I managed to climb onto the roof. I hated that the simple climb made me breathe so heavily. I sat next to Sam, my brothers, and my father, heard another explosion, and way off in the distance, we could see tiny spots of red and green.

"There it is!" exclaimed Jeremy.

Then my mother gave up and came onto the roof, too, and sat next to my dad. Some faint yellow lights appeared and we cheered; this continued for a while until the finale lit up the distant sky. We all sat there for a few minutes, feeling the warm summer breeze and enjoying the moment. Finally, my mom got up and said the only words that could get us all off the roof: "Time for dessert!"

"I made Harry's Flag Cake," my dad bragged as we walked into the house. Harry was an old friend of my dad's, and on Memorial Day, July Fourth, and Labor Day, he always made a flag cake, basically a sheet cake covered with whipped cream and using strawberries and blueberries for the stars and stripes. It was our favorite cake, and my brothers and I fought every time over who got the piece with all the blueberries.

We laughed as we made our way into the kitchen, and Jeremy got out the plates while my dad took the milk out of the fridge. Mom always insisted that if you were going to have pastry, you had to have milk.

But as I got a few forks out of the silverware drawer, I heard a beep.

"Did someone put something in the microwave?" I asked, going over to check; it was empty. We brought everything to the table and sat down, and Dad made a production of getting the knife out and trying to figure out how to cut the cake. And then we heard another beep.

"It's not the microwave. Did someone set another timer?" my mother asked.

"Is it someone's cell phone?" my dad wondered.

"The beeper!" I exclaimed, running over to the counter where the hospital beeper sat. "Oh my God, how long has this been going off?"

If they couldn't find me, they might give the heart to someone else. I pushed the button to see the hospital phone number come up: the call had come in only ten minutes earlier. Then I grabbed the phone and started to dial. *Here we go again,* I thought, as I pushed the numbers.

"Do you want me to call?" my mom offered.

"No, I can do it." I dialed without the slightest bit of hesitation.

"Hello, this is Emmi Miller. Hi, Nancy." I tried to

steady my breathing along with my shaking hands. "Wow, that's great. We're coming right in." I turned to my family. "They have a heart."

Sam came up behind me and put his arms around me.

My mom took charge: "I'm going to get a few things together. Dan, can you get the magazines on my dresser?"

"What if this one doesn't work out either?" I asked.

"It will. And if it doesn't, we'll wait again. But I have a good feeling this time, Emmi. Go get your bag," Mom said.

Sam and I went upstairs together; he sat on my bed while I threw pajamas into my duffle. I used to have my bag packed and ready, but a month ago I got so frustrated, I unpacked everything. I sat down on the bed next to Sam and put my head on his shoulder.

"You're going to be fine," he said.

"How'd you know what I was thinking?" I asked.

"We're going to Mongolia to teach little kids, right? Don't forget—we've got a plan."

"Take good care of my brothers."

"We'll have some fun tonight."

"No, I mean—if—you know, if anything happens to me."

"Em, nothing's going to happen. You're going to have this surgery and you're going to feel better. And then you're going to get your normal life back." I was glad at least one of us was feeling confident. Part of me thought everything would go fine, but the realistic part knew it might not.

I put my head on his chest for a minute; listening to his heart beating made me realize how badly mine was working. Then we stood up.

"I'm going to go do this." We looked into his eyes; he smiled my favorite Sam-smile.

"I love you," he whispered. He'd never said that before and I stared at him. Then he leaned down and kissed me.

"I love you, too," I said.

"See you tomorrow," Sam said.

And I believed him.

37

This time things were calmer on the way to the hospital. My father took the parkway, driving with purpose but not the "get out of my way" anxiety my mom had the first time. I called Becca but she didn't answer (where was she at this time of night?), so I left a message telling her what was about to happen. I asked her not to come back to New York—she had only two days of camp left and I didn't want to ruin it for her.

Finally at the hospital, as we walked into the lobby, my mother again took my hand. And like last time, I was glad. We took the elevator to the Heart Center, and this time I had no problem getting off the elevator and going to the desk with my mother. After all these months of feeling lousy, with my whole life on hold, I was eager to get this over with.

It was such déjà vu when the same blonde nurse led us down the hall to that same exam room where I put on the same colorless cloth gown.

"Dr. Leavens isn't on call this weekend, honey," my blonde nurse said. "But she'll come by tomorrow."

"What about Dr. Harrison?" I asked. "Is he here?"

"Yes, he is, and he'll come by in a few minutes," she said. I liked Dr. Harrison, if for no other reason than he reminded me of Sam. And he was very confident; being as nervous as I was, I needed my doctor to be confident. Then came a knock on the door and Dr. Harrison walked in. He was tan now and his hair was lighter; he was even cuter than last time.

"Hi, Emmi. How're you doing?" he asked.

"I don't know. Ready to get this over with, I guess." Actually, I was amazed at how calm I was. This time I felt excited, anticipating-something-good feelings, not the huge dread and worry I'd nearly drowned in lately.

"I had a feeling we were going to see you this weekend. Unfortunately, with all of the car accidents on holiday weekends, that's when we get an increase in available organs."

"That's horrible to think about," I said.

"It's always sad when a family loses someone, but it does make us feel slightly better to know their loss can be used to save someone else's life."

"It's still a weird concept. Some kid has to die so I can live—I hate it."

Dr. Harrison nodded at me. There was nothing left to say, really.

"The team went to Long Island to check the heart and it looks great. They're heading back with it now, so as long as your blood tests are fine, we're going to get you ready for surgery. Sound good?" He smiled, and there was the Sam-smile again.

"I'm ready." Did he expect me to say no?

"I'll see you when it's all over." Then he walked out of the room.

"Some kid probably went to the beach and got drunk," my father said. We weren't allowed to know who the donor was—which was probably for the best. I already felt guilty enough about the whole thing; I didn't want to know anything else.

My blonde nurse came back in, carrying a steel tray with needles and vials on it.

"Let me take your temperature first," she said. After I got a perfect 98.6, she stuck me and drew some blood. She filled three vials, all with different color caps. They had to make sure I wasn't sick or anything before they gave me the heart. These tests made the SATs seem like a piece of cake. After all, if I did lousy on the SATs, I could still go to college. But if I didn't do well on my blood tests, well . . . my mind was wandering.

The nurse took the vials of blood and left the room.

"It feels like things are moving along faster this time," my mom said.

"We never got to have the flag cake," my dad realized.

"I'm sure the boys are eating it," I said.

"I'll make you your own flag cake when you get home," my dad said. "Then you won't have to fight your brothers for the blueberries."

"It was fun going up on the roof tonight," I said.

"It'll definitely go in the Miller Classic Fourth of July Hall of Fame," Mom said. The door opened and it was my blonde nurse.

"Okay! They're ready for you, honey," she said.

"Omigod." I took in a breath and held it. Then my mom took my hand and I exhaled

"You're going to do great," my mom said.

I ignored the tears in her eyes; I wasn't letting my mind go anywhere negative. We were marching forward—this was finally happening!

My nurse wheeled in a gurney, the beds on wheels they use to transport patients.

"Hop on up," my nurse said and I climbed on to the gurney.

"Do you have my stuff?" I asked my parents.

"Don't worry, honey. We've got everything," my mom answered.

"Lie with your head on the pillow," my nurse instructed. "We'll keep your meds going through your pump for now, but that'll be taken out during the surgery. I'm going to put a line into the other arm for the sedative and you'll just feel a slight pinch," she said as she put the needle into my arm.

"Okay, honey, now I'm going to start sedation. I want you to list everything you can think that you love, all your favorite things. Just start listing them."

"Out loud, or to myself?" I asked.

"However you like."

Then my parents came over and each gave me a kiss.

"See you soon," Mom whispered.

"Call the boys and make sure they haven't eaten my whole cake," I said to her.

"Good idea," she said, smiling through her tears.

"Tell Sam I said hi."

I started my list: *Mom, Dad, Jeremy, Eli, soccer, Becca, comfortable sweats, flag cakes, Sam, Sam's eyes.*

He said he loved me. . . .

Part 2

38

I'm alive! Omigod, I'm alive—at least I thought I was. My head felt fuzzy and I was too tired to move. I tried to pinch my leg to see if I felt anything.

"She's moving. She's pinching her leg," I heard someone say. Was it my mother? I tried to speak, but I couldn't find my voice. "Why is she pinching her leg?" Mom asked. Someone took my hand. I needed to open my eyes, to say something, but I was having trouble. I decided to sleep for a few more minutes.

"Emmi, it's Mommy, can you hear me?" "Mommy"? I hadn't called her that since I was six. I knew I needed to answer her and tried to form the words, but it wasn't happening, so I squeezed her hand. "You're okay, Emmi. You came through it just great."

The brain-fuzz was lifting a little and I was able to open my eyes. I'd made it! I hadn't died on the table. And now I had some other kid's heart beating in my chest. I could feel the pulsing, perfect beat of my strong new heart. It was too much to think about.

"Dan, her eyes are open. Emmi, hi. How are you?" I tried again to answer my mother but couldn't manage it.

"Emmi, you can't talk. You've got a breathing tube," my dad said. He leaned over and kissed me on the forehead. "I love you, honey."

"Stop kissing her, Dan," my mom scolded. "We're not supposed to get that close yet—germs!"

"I can't help it," my dad said. "I'm so happy to see her."

I looked around the room.

"There's no one else here," Mom said, guessing what I was thinking. "You're only allowed two visitors at a time in the ICU. Sam's home with your brothers."

What time was it? What day was it? How much had I missed? I tried to ask the time, but my hands felt heavy and I seemed to have more tubes and wires coming out of me than I ever expected. Where were all these tubes going?

A nurse came in and looked over at me. "Ah, Emmi, you're awake. Hi." She hustled through the room in her teddy-bear-covered scrubs. I could hear the clomping of her clogs on the floor as she walked over to my bed, bringing a small cart with squeaky wheels that made my teeth hurt. She took my blood pressure; none of these tubes or wires was able to do that? There was a clip at the end of my finger and it glowed red; even though I felt like ET, it was awesome.

"That measures the oxygen in your blood," the nurse explained. "I'm Patty, by the way. I'll be your day-shift nurse." I tried to smile in response. "Don't worry, we'll get that tube out in a little while, as soon as we get the okay from Dr. Harrison." I managed a tiny nod; I was tired and closed my eyes again.

The next time I opened them, the room was much darker. My mom was sitting and flipping through a magazine, a small light on over her head. I tried to get her attention, but she wasn't looking my way. I moved my legs to rustle the sheet and she looked over.

"Hi," she said. "You slept a long time."

"I know," I said. The tube was out—I could talk! "Where's Dad?"

"He went home to the boys."

"I'm thirsty and my throat's killing me."

"They say that happens—from the breathing tube." She brought me a cup of water and put the straw to my lips and the cool water felt soothing. Then I saw a tall figure at the door and assumed it was Dr. Harrison, checking in on me. But when he stepped into the room, I realized it was Sam. No—I didn't want him to see me like this! I must look awful.

"Go away," I said, shielding my face from his sight. My tubes got tangled and I wasn't able to bring my right hand up to my face. My mom came over to the bed to attempt to free me. "You can't see me like this," I told him.

Sam came closer and I could see the worry in his eyes.

"How are you?" he asked.

"I'm here," I said.

"Yeah," he said, still staring and not smiling. What was

up with him? "You look much better than you did yesterday," he said.

Yesterday? How long have I been out? They let him see me like that?

"Wash your hands, Sam," my mother said.

"Oh—sorry, I forgot," Sam said, going over to the sink and working up a lather. When he was done, he came over to the bed.

"What day is it?" I demanded.

"It's Saturday, July sixth," my mother answered.

"July sixth?" I asked. *I lost two days?* "What happened?"

"You had some bleeding after your surgery. They had to go back in and repair it," Mom explained.

"Another surgery? But I don't remember. I didn't—"

"Sshh, Em. They kept you sedated to rest your body. But there *was* a point where we thought we might lose you."

"Am I okay now?"

Sam looked over at my mother.

"Dr. Leavens thinks we're past the crisis," she said.

The crisis? There was a crisis?

"What happens now?" Sam asked. His seriousness worried me.

"Well, we wait. We keep an eye on Emmi and test her blood levels to make sure she's not rejecting the heart. Dr. Leavens'll explain more when she comes in the morning."

"What time is it?" I asked.

"Eight-ten—only twenty more minutes left for visiting hours," a voice said from the door. Becca!

"What happened to camp?" I asked.

"It ended this morning so I drove all day to see you. Hey, your hair looks great." I just had a crisis and Becca was still giving it to me.

"Becca, you need to wash your hands," Mom said. She truly was the germ police around here. Becca did as she was told and scrubbed.

Then a nurse poked her head into the room. "I'm sorry, only two visitors at a time in ICU. The hospital's very strict about this," she informed us. My mom looked at Becca, who looked at Sam, who looked at my mom.

"I just got here," Becca said.

"I'm the boyfriend," Sam said.

"And I'm the mom, who trumps the boyfriend," my mother said. "Oh, never mind, I've been here all day. I could use a little walk. Enjoy your visitors, Emmi." She grabbed her bag and headed out the door.

"How was camp?" I asked Becca.

"Who cares? How are you?"

"I don't know, tired. A little bit freaked out. They said I was in pain before, but I don't really remember it. Mostly, I'm tired." Sam walked over to the door. Was he trying to leave? Was this whole thing too much for him? Becca wasn't wrong—I was a mess. Maybe seeing me like this changed his mind about me.

"Have my brothers been here yet?" I asked Sam.

"No. Your mom didn't think they could handle it, seeing you with all the tubes and everything." Could Sam?

"But it was okay to let you come?"

"I guess," he said.

"Maybe the boys can come when I get out of the ICU. My friend Abe said he was walking the day after surgery and out of the ICU in two days," I told them.

"Wow," said Becca.

"Abe?" asked Sam. "What is he, like, eighty?"

"No, he's our age."

"Who is he?" Sam asked.

"This guy I met. He had a transplant two years ago."

"So when were you talking to him?" Sam asked.

"I don't know. A few times before my surgery."

"Do you hang out?" Sam wasn't letting this go, but he didn't have anything to worry about.

"No, it's nothing like that. You know I love you."

"How come you didn't tell me?" Sam asked.

"There wasn't anything to tell. I don't give you a list of everyone I speak to."

"Yeah, but—"

"But what?"

"I don't know," he said. "It's different."

"Why? Because he's a guy? So what? I needed to talk to someone."

"You could have talked to me."

"I did. But it's different when it's someone who's been through it." Didn't Sam know he had nothing to worry about?

"Get off her case, Sam. It's no big deal," Becca said.

"I think I'm entitled to know if she's hanging out with other guys," Sam said.

"This is *not* a big deal," I shouted, hurting my throat. "I'm tired, Sam. I can't fight with you. I'm sorry if I have a friend who's a guy." I looked at Sam and our eyes met. He just shook his head.

"You could have told me," Sam said. "I'm sorry, Em. It's been a hard couple of days."

"Yeah—for me, too, don't you think?"

"Hey, I had a hard couple of days, too. And I drove ten hours straight—and only stopped to pee once," Becca said.

"Oh yeah, you're right. That's much harder than having your chest cracked open and your heart replaced and a second surgery and almost dying. You definitely win," I said.

The nurse walked into the room. "Visiting hours are over, kids. Time to go," she said.

As nice as it was for them to come, part of me was relieved they were leaving—I was exhausted just from talking to them.

I closed my eyes and barely heard them go.

39

The next thing I remember, it was light out again and Dr. Leavens was leaning over me. My mom was next to her; she looked a little crumpled. Ah, the dreaded bed-chair. I had vague memories of Sam and Becca visiting, but mostly the past few days were a blur.

"Hi, Emmi. How are you doing?" Dr. Leavens asked.

"Okay, I think. Right?" I asked her. *Please say yes.*

"Actually you're doing great. You're already off the ventilator and breathing on your own, which is important. I'd like you to try to get out of bed today."

"But I'm barely sitting up."

"Try to sit up in bed this morning. And see if you can eat a little. Then, in the afternoon, we can try to let you sit in the chair."

"I never imagined my big achievement of the day would be getting up and sitting in a chair."

"What about all of the wires?" my mom asked. *Good question.*

"We'll be taking a few more out this morning. She won't need the IV if she starts eating and drinking. The rest we can maneuver if we move the chair closer to the bed," Dr. Leavens said.

"The sooner I sit, the sooner I walk, right? The sooner I walk, the sooner I can get out of the hospital? When I'm out of the hospital, I can start training for soccer, right?" I wanted to move this thing forward.

"Slow down a little," Dr. Leavens said. "Let's take the small steps first. And we still have to monitor you and make sure you're not rejecting the heart. You're going to be here at least a week or two more. Let's take it day by day and see how it goes. Then we can work on your training schedule."

"I'm going to be back on that field for the fall," I told Dr. Leavens and my mother. Didn't they get how important this was to me?

"Emmi, I don't know," my mom said.

"Again, Emmi, let's go slow," Dr. Leavens said. "I'm thrilled that you have a goal, but we also need to be a little conservative."

"And protective," my mother added.

"We don't want you in big crowds for a couple of months," Dr. Leavens said.

"The soccer field's not a crowd," I protested. "And you can't get germs outside. They disperse in the air too quickly."

"Let's work on getting you in the chair today. We'll worry about soccer another time," the doctor replied.

She was probably right. But I wanted to think about getting back to the soccer field; I *needed* to think about it. It was the only thing getting me through all this.

As the hospital stay dragged on, I felt good enough to become bored. I left the ICU five days after my surgery and there were no major complications or rejection—so far.

Sam and Becca did not come back and visit after that first day in the ICU; in fact, they both were being a little distant and I didn't know why. Becca said she had a cold and didn't want to give it to me, but she sounded fine so I knew that wasn't it and had no idea what was wrong. As for Sam . . . I didn't know. Maybe he was busy with camp.

When I was in a regular room, the Child Life Center lent me a laptop computer again. My mom or dad was there during the day, but it got lonely at night and it was good to have the computer for company. I went online to search colleges and to find good conditioning exercises for soccer training. There was even a support group for teens with heart transplants. And I was able to be on Facebook as much as I wanted. Sam and Becca weren't on much but Abe was. I sort of benefited from his "no job, no friends" summer.

Abe:	*So how's the new ticker?*
Emmi:	*OK so far.*
Abe:	*Do you feel different?*
Emmi:	*Not as tired, which is nice. Did you?*
Abe:	*Happier. Maybe the kid I got my heart from was nicer than me.*
Emmi:	*You don't believe all that, do you? That you become like that person?*
Abe:	*Maybe.*

Emmi: *That's impossible. It's just a muscle, there's no emotion or thought in muscle.*

Abe: *It's hard to explain, but there are times I think I'm feeling things I've never felt before.*

Emmi: *Yeah. They call that puberty.*

Abe: *Ha ha. And the chicks dig me much more since my surgery.*

Emmi: *That's called pity ☺.*

Abe: *Ouch! Maybe the person you got your heart from was kind of bitchy.*

Emmi: *Nope, I was that way b 4, too. Now you know.*

❧

Abe: *Have your first biopsy yet?*

Emmi: *Yes. OUCH!*

Abe: *Get used 2 it. It's going 2 B every week for a while.*

Emmi: *They don't make it easy.*

Abe: *Rejection's a big worry. For the rest of your life.*

Emmi: *That's cheery.*

Abe: *I didn't invent the rules; I just play by them.*

❧

Emmi: *So where'd you get the name "Abe"?*

Abe: *Don't you like it?*

Emmi: *It's great. But unusual for a 16-year-old.*

Abe: *I was named for my grandfather, who died before I was born.*

Emmi: *I was named for old dead people, too. Esther, Marty, Miriam and Irving. They took the first letter from each of their names.*

Abe: *One more thing we have in common! Do u believe in soul mates?*

Emmi: *I have a boyfriend, Abe.*

Abe: *o*

Emmi: *But I luv being friends with u. Please don't b mad.*

Abe: *He's a lucky guy. Is he one of those hot jock guys?*

Emmi: *Sort of. I guess.*

Abe: *I guess that beats skinny and funny.*

Emmi: *Skinny and funny's good, too. I need u as my friend, Abe.*

Abe: *Yeah, I'm getting pretty used to u 2.*

Emmi: *I'm getting out of here 2morrow. It's been less than 2 weeks. Not a record, but not bad.*

Abe: *It's still a long road, but you've gotten thru a big part. Will u still write to me when u r home?*

Emmi: *Of course. Besides, didn't u say it's going 2 be a boring 2 months before I get back to school? What else would I do?*

40

"Emmi, time for your meds," my mom shouted from downstairs. The school district gave her a few weeks off to take care of me when I got out of the hospital.

"I took them," I shouted back. In my effort to become the best posttransplant patient ever, I was always conscious of when I needed to take my pills. We decided it was best to take them at eleven a.m. and eleven p.m. every day. That way I could sleep late and not have to wake up to take them. It was also the senior class lunchtime, so it'd fit in perfectly on school days.

My mom poked her head into my room. "Ready to walk?" she asked.

Every day since I got home, we'd taken a walk around the neighborhood, going farther and farther each day. We were already up to three miles.

"Why don't we walk around the lake?" Mom asked. "Might be a nice change."

"I don't know."

"Why not? Aren't you bored with walking circles around our neighborhood?"

"I'm not sure I'm ready to be in public yet." I started untying and tying my sneaker laces.

"Emmi, what's wrong?" Mom asked. She got down on the floor next to my sneakers and put her hand over the laces. "Talk to me."

"I don't look like myself. I've got this steroid 'moon face.' I'm like a distorted version of my old self." There— I'd said it. I'd been thinking about it all last week. Abe had warned me, but I didn't think it would happen to me; the steroids that prevent rejection made my face swell.

"I don't think it's so bad," she said.

"But you're my mother. As in 'a face only a mother could love.' "

She stood up and went over to my dresser, took a pair of my wide sunglasses, and handed them to me. "Put these on," she said. "Maybe it won't be as noticeable."

I put the glasses on; I still looked puffy, but maybe it wasn't as obvious.

"We've heard this could go on for a while, and you'll have to get used to it. Your friends will understand and be supportive."

"Have you met my friends? And what about the other kids in school? They tease people for a lot less. I can imagine the nicknames they'll come up with."

"You've gotten through everything else; it's one more thing," Mom said. I hated when she got all philosophical on me.

"Yeah, but this one's so *obvious*."

She started to say something.

"And don't say it's what's inside that counts. High school students are much too shallow to believe that."

We drove over to Rockland Lake. "We used to run around the lake to get in shape for soccer season," I said. "The path's about three miles."

"We should have gone earlier. It's getting hot," Mom said.

"I brought water bottles. We'll be fine."

We got out of the car, stretched a little, and started walking. The lake was beautiful; the sun was shining at an angle that made the water sparkle. Geese were swimming around and occasionally waddling ashore to snatch some bread from the children tossing it to them. The walking path was crowded with mothers pushing carriages, people strolling, power walking, or jogging, and an occasional bicyclist or rollerblader. The biggest obstacle was the piles of goose poop scattered on the ground; Mom and I kept a pretty good pace, but I was almost run down by a bicyclist as I dodged some pretty nasty goose poop and strayed into his path. But then some hot guys in spandex running shorts and tank tops jogged by, making up for it.

"Nice buns!" Mom said.

"Mom. I cannot discuss nice buns with you."

"And I thought we were bonding."

"There are some things that are just too weird to talk about with your mother."

"Can I ask you how things are with Sam? It doesn't seem like you're talking much."

"We text every once in a while. He's at camp all day and I think the kids really wear him out."

"Is that what he told you?" she asked.

"No, but I can't imagine why he wouldn't call more."

"Why don't you invite him over?" she asked, taking another sip of water. I reached for my water bottle, too. It was at least eighty-five degrees and I didn't want to get dehydrated.

"I don't want him to see me puffy. And I thought you said no one could come over."

"You can hang out outside. But no kissing."

"Hmm, that's tough. What about holding hands?"

"Only if you wash your hands afterward, with antibacterial soap."

"Boy, you are paranoid," I said. I was starting to get a little winded, but I wanted to keep pushing myself. We were about three-quarters of the way around the lake, and Mom was breathing heavily, too.

"Are you okay?" she asked me, taking a swig of water.

"I'm fine—great. Let's keep going." I picked up the pace till we could see the parking lot and I broke into a sprint. Mom sprinted, too, and beat me to the car.

I'd definitely have to work on that.

41

That night I turned on my computer to find Sam logged on.

Emmi: *Hey.*

Sam: *Hey. Sup?*

Emmi: *Good news. Mom says u can come over.*

I waited what felt like a very long minute—or two. Maybe he went to the bathroom or something.

Emmi: *u there?*

Another minute passed. Should I be worried about this?

Sam: *Hi. Yeah, I'm here. My mom was talking to me for a sec.*

Emmi: *So do you want to come over? May b for dinner 2morrow?*

Sam: *Can't do dinner. Late night at camp.*

Emmi: *How were the brats today?*

Sam: *Brattier than ever. How r u feeling?*

Emmi: *Mom and I walked the lake today. I'm going to start running next week.*

Sam: *Sounds like a good plan.*

Emmi: *So come by after ur late night 2morrow.*

Sam: *Don't know. Might be tired.*

Emmi: *Come on! We can finally see each other! O—Mom says no kissing.*

Sam: *I know. I'm a big germ to her.*

Emmi: *I'm calling u on ur cell 2morrow on ur way home. I'm going to hound you until you get over here.*

Sam: *Pushy, pushy girl.*

Emmi: *I miss u.*

Sam: *Miss u 2.*

Emmi: *Sam?*

Sam: *What?*

Emmi: *I look different.*

Sam: *So?*

Emmi: *My face is puffy. I don't look like me. Side effect of my meds.*

Sam: *No biggie. Ur still u, right?*

Emmi: *u say all the right things.*

It was nice of him to say, but he hadn't seen my face yet.

42

I talked Eli into "coaching" me back into shape. Well, I didn't talk him into it; I offered to pay him. What had this world come to when I had to bribe my little brother to play soccer with me? We started with easy drills, stuff like dribbling around the cone. I was definitely much weaker than before I got sick, but I was optimistic that I'd get back in shape.

The exercise kept me distracted, but I was impatient to see Sam. At seven-thirty I called him on his cell.

"Hi. When are you coming over?" I asked.

"I don't know, Em. I'm tired."

"I finally got permission for you to come over. Come say hi, even if it's just for fifteen minutes." Silence. "Please?"

"Okay, okay, I'm coming over," he said.

We hung up. I ran upstairs to check my hair and clothes. It was the first time he was seeing me since the surgery. Well, since the ICU. I certainly couldn't look any worse than I did that day. I looked in the mirror: a big moon face stared back at me. What was he going to think? Would he still like me? Even though my color was better than before I got the heart, I put on a little extra blush and some lip gloss just to be safe. My hair was typically hopeless, but I pulled it back in a ponytail and left a little strand out. Sam always liked when that little strand stuck out. Did my face look worse with my hair pulled back? I took it out and put it up again. I just couldn't tell.

The longest ten minutes of my life ended when the doorbell rang. I opened the door and jumped into Sam's arms, burying my face in his shoulder, delaying him from seeing my moon face.

"What happened to 'no contact/no germs'?" he asked, smiling shyly.

"You're right. Go wash up." He did, and then he came out wiping his hands on one of the disposable towels my mother put in the bathroom. She didn't even want to take chances leaving a regular towel there, in case it harbored some hidden bacteria.

I grabbed Sam's hand and kissed it. "It's great to see you. I've missed you so much," I said. He gave me a half-smile but didn't say anything. Was it my face? "Do I look totally weird?" I asked him.

"No, just a little puffy—but still you," he said. He didn't sound convincing.

I took his hand and said, "It's a beautiful night; let's sit outside. And besides, my mother believes there's less chance of spreading germs outside." We went out the back door and sat on the patio swing. But Sam was being unusually quiet.

"How's camp?" I asked.

"Fine. Same." One-word answers—what was up with that? He must think I look awful.

"Sam, before my surgery, you'd have paragraphs of comments on each kid. What's different now?"

"Nothing, really." Sam looked at me and made eye contact for the first time that night; I'd forgotten how much I loved those green-gold eyes. We started to lean in to each other to kiss, but I backed off quickly, realizing we shouldn't.

"This is torture," I said. "Is that why you haven't come by? Maybe you were right."

"No. I— Oh, Emmi," he sighed.

"What?" He looked so sad. "I'm okay now—at least so far. Another biopsy tomorrow, but I feel great. I can't imagine I'm rejecting."

But he still looked sad—almost distracted.

"Sam, what's wrong?" He looked at me, started to say something, but then changed his mind.

"I'm fine. Just tired I guess."

"That's a switch—you're the tired one. Why don't you go home? You can come by another day." He looked almost relieved.

"Yeah—I think I will. I'm sorry, Em."

"No biggie. I'm glad I got to see you for a few minutes," I said, not sure I meant it. Something was definitely off.

We walked to his car and he got in. I wanted a good-bye kiss so badly; something to make me feel like everything was normal. But we couldn't and he just drove away. As I watched his car go down the street, I felt very empty and alone. He was the first friend I had seen in the two weeks I'd been home, and he didn't even stay for ten minutes.

Was this the same guy who came to see me when I was unconscious? Who told me he loved me? Could he not deal with the puffy version of me? Did I do or say something in the hospital to offend him? I couldn't imagine. I went inside and tried to call Becca; she wasn't home so I called her cell: no answer.

I went upstairs to the computer and no one was on—not even an acquaintance. I called Abe, who was always available, and couldn't even reach him on his cell. Where was everybody? Did everyone have a life but me?

I walked over to my wall and looked at all of the collages. My life had always been full of action and people and fun. How did this all happen to me? I wasn't a bad person. I wasn't one of the mean girls who're horrible to other girls just because of what they wear or how they look. I once gave my seat to an old lady on the subway when Becca and I were in the city. I could be a little bitchy to my mom, but I didn't do drugs and I took good care of myself. Why me? Now even my boyfriend found me too pitiful and boring and ugly to hang out with.

My life truly sucked.

43

There was a part of me the next morning that didn't want to take my meds. What did I have to live for? Soccer seemed like a distant dream, my boyfriend was uncomfortable in my presence, and my friends were too busy for me. I picked up the stack of pills and held them over the toilet bowl. I could drop them in and flush them away and no one would be the wiser. Would the doctors even know if I didn't take them? Would anyone even care? I held the pills high above the bowl, willing myself to do it.

"Emmi, what are you doing?" Eli asked me. I jumped; I hadn't known he was there.

"Nothing! Why?" I clenched my fist around the pills.

"Mom! Emmi was about to flush her pills!" he shouted down the stairs. That brought my mother running.

"Don't you have soccer camp or band camp or something to go to?" I asked him, annoyed.

"What? Emmi, what the hell are you doing?" she asked, breathing heavily from her sprint up the stairs.

"Nothing. I don't know what you're all getting so excited about," I said, as blasé as possible. "I was about to take my eleven a.m. meds."

Then my mom did something totally strange. She hugged me. And she started crying. "I'm so sorry, kiddo," she said through her tears. That did it. I started crying, too. Deep sobs. The events of the past months were swirling around in my head as the tears ran down my face.

I let Mom hold me for a few minutes and then we pulled apart. She grabbed a piece of toilet paper and ripped off a piece for both of us. We blew our noses in unison. "Enough crying. This pity party is over," she said. "From here on it's all positive. Up and out. You're going to be fine."

My cell rang and I grabbed it. I got the tears out of my voice and said my chirpiest, "Hello."

"Emmi, it's me, Abe."

"Hi, Abe. What's up?"

"Do you have a biopsy today?" he asked.

"Yeah, why?"

"I got my mom to switch my appointment. I'll be at the hospital today, too. Let's have lunch." He sounded so excited; it was hard to say no.

"I need to ask my mom."

"She can meet my mom. I bet they'll have a lot to talk about." It was great to hear his voice. At my lowest point, he was exactly what I needed to put one foot in front of the other and move out the door. "You think they'd do side-by-side biopsies?"

"Oh yeah, I'm sure the doctors would love that." I laughed at the picture of him holding my hand while two doctors performed the biopsies. *Holding my hand? Did I just think that? Is that too familiar? Is that a "more than friends" kind of thing?* My face felt warm and I was glad he couldn't see me. And *really* glad Sam couldn't see me. I felt guilty about the momentary disloyalty. "I'll ask my mom in the car and let you know when I see you."

"Tell her I'd be eternally grateful," he said.

"Yeah, she was hoping she could have your eternal gratitude. It's the one thing she's missing in her life."

44

When I saw Abe in the waiting room, I realized his face was roundish, too. Because I didn't know him before his transplant, it never struck me as unusual. We hadn't seen each other since my transplant, though we had texted or spoken so often it felt like we had. He was wearing a band T-shirt that said LYNYRD SKYNYRD and baggy cargo shorts. Seeing me, he walked across the waiting room and started to lift his shirt.

"Flashing me is not an acceptable greeting," I told him.

"But it gives me such pleasure," he said.

"Find another outlet for your pleasure." We smiled at each other. I really liked this guy. But was it "like" or was it "like like"? And how could I "like like" him when I loved Sam? Abe put his arm around my shoulder and gave it a squeeze.

"How's your sternum?" he asked.

"That's a very forward question," I said, laughing.

"I didn't ask to *see* your sternum. That would be a forward question." He leaned in closer. "But if you're offering . . . ," he whispered and winked.

I punched him in the shoulder. "You wish." *Does he wish? Do I wish? What's happening here?*

My mother had agreed to lunch. We went to my favorite hospital spot, a café in the lobby. I got my usual, a hummus and veggie wrap. Mom got one, too, though she often liked the soups. Abe and his mother had their favorites, too. We all knew the menu by heart—definitely a product of having eaten there way too many times.

Our moms chatted like old friends; I'd been so focused on how great it was to have Abe to talk to, it didn't occur to me that my mom might need someone, too—someone who'd been through the same thing. She seemed so relaxed, and I could hear Jane answering a lot of her questions. Jane was a slightly chubby, aging hippie type, someone my mom would call an Upper West Side intellectual. She wore a long skirt with a blouse and sandals, and she was one of the few moms I'd met who didn't dye her hair. My mom looked like a teenager next to her.

"So what's Lynyrd Skynyrd?" I asked Abe, pointing to his T-shirt.

" 'What's Lynyrd Skynyrd'? Only the most awesome southern rock band of all time."

"You're into southern rock?"

"Yeah, and a lot of other '70s rock bands."

"I wondered why you were always wearing old band T-shirts."

"Nothing gets by you," he said. "You know Skynyrd was singing about social injustice and the environment long before it was cool. So much of today's music is nothing but fluff and a lot of screaming."

"I don't know if I agree," I said, determined to defend my generation's music. "Look at—umm . . ." I couldn't come up with a good example.

"Yeah, how many songs that you've listened to lately were actually written by the people who are performing them?"

"I'm sure I can come up with someone; but that's our parents' music—why would you want to listen to that?" I asked.

"Because it's your parents' that means it's bad?"

"Yeah, it's called adolescent rebellion. We can't be seen liking what our parents like. It's not cool."

"You're having the same lunch as your mother. Is that also not cool?"

"That's food. It's different."

"Maybe I'm just above the insecurities of cool and un-cool," he said, folding his arms across his chest. "I listen to what I like."

"So do I."

"Good."

"Good." We sat in silence for a moment. I finished my wrap and took another sip of water. I tried to think of a singer I liked who wrote his own music—nothing. It's possible there was one, but I hadn't paid that much attention. Was I shallow? It never occurred to me to think about the songwriting and the story behind the music.

"Why is this so important to you?" I asked.

"My dad was a roadie for a lot of these bands. That's where I got all of my T-shirts. They were from tours that he worked on."

I leaned in closer. This was cool. "What did he do for them?"

"He was an engineer and did sound for them."

"Does he still do that?" I asked, thinking maybe we could score some hot concert tickets. "Is that why I've never met him?"

"He left when I was three. Wanted to go back on the road. He'd been doing it for so many years, he didn't think he could function without it. Mom refused to go along with it, so he left."

"He left his wife and kid to go on the road? Who does that?"

Abe nodded and took a bite of his sandwich.

"Does he know everything you've been going through?" I asked.

"He died in a bus accident when I was five."

"How can you say this all so calmly?" I asked. He continued eating, like this was no big deal.

"Emmi, it was ten years ago. We're past all the drama."

"So the music is your way of having a piece of him."

"Thanks, Freud," he said. "Tell me something I haven't thought of."

"Do you play, too?" I asked him.

"No, we live in an apartment building. Thin walls and cranky neighbors don't mix with rock and roll. But I do a cool music blog. I'll show you sometime." He crumpled up the wrapper to his sandwich and shot it into a nearby garbage can—it went in. "Score! See, Sam's not the only athlete you hang with."

"Call me and I'll come watch your next garbage-can basketball game."

The moms had finished their lunch and were ready to go.

"Jane, thank you so much for this," my mom said, hugging her new friend.

Abe gave me the sideways shoulder squeeze again and whispered, "We'll go for the frontal hug when you're healed some more."

"You've given me something to live for," I said, laughing.

Though in a way there was some truth to it. Mom and I walked over to the valet parking and Abe and Jane headed toward the subway entrance. Who would've thought my biopsy day would bring me the most fun I'd had since my surgery?

I thought about Abe and how brave he was, and how much he must have missed his dad. And how his mother had to go through everything alone. Mom was right; the pity party was over. I had plenty to live for, if for nothing more than the chance to get a frontal hug from Abe. The thought of it made me blush and then made me feel guilty about blushing.

I didn't know what was up with Sam, but I did know that I loved him and hoped that when things got back to normal, everything would be fine between us.

45

On my six-week anniversary, I decided to try running. Dr. Leavens said to go for it, and although I'd been walking several miles every day at a brisk pace, I hadn't tried a full run yet.

"Let me come with you," my mother said.

"No, Mom. I want to go alone."

"What if something happens?" she asked.

"Nothing's going to happen. And I have my cell with me, just in case." I strapped on the armband my dad got me for my iPod—there's nothing better than running to great tunes, and I'd downloaded a few of the bands Abe was raving about and really liked them, too. Some of the songs were perfect for running and I'd put together an hour-long playlist.

"Make it a short run, okay?" my mom said.

"Mom, I'll be fine. If I'm not, I'll slow down and walk." I put the ear buds in and pushed Play. "I'll be back soon."

I ran down my street; it was a great neighborhood for

running, flat and without much traffic. I figured I'd do one of my old runs, through the streets at first and then into a nearby park and through the woods, where there were usually enough people on the path to make it safe.

I'd called Becca to see if she wanted to run with me, but she and Noelle had plans to go to the city, so neither one of them could run with me. Lauren decided to go on the European soccer trip that Becca and I'd done last year—those European guys had no idea what they were in for once Lauren showed up. Every few days I'd get a postcard from her with nothing but a number on it; I was guessing it was the number of guys she'd kissed—or more? I was sure I'd get all the gory details when she got back.

Becca seemed to be hanging with Noelle a lot lately and part of me was coming to accept they were much closer now. Becca'd been my BFF for so long that I took it for granted, and I couldn't say I blamed them—it hadn't been much fun to be with me lately. Summer was for going to the beach and hanging out, and I couldn't do any of those things. My mom had said I could have them over, but they always seemed to be busy when I called. Were they avoiding me? Abe said the same thing happened to him after his transplant, but once he got back to school things got back to normal.

Sam and I texted or spoke every day, but something was definitely off between us—things just didn't seem right. Was it me? But I didn't seem to have that problem with Abe. We spent hours texting, talking, and even having video chats; it felt like I'd known him forever.

I got to the park part of my run just in time for a great song by Paul McCartney. Abe not only listened to these songs, but he knew the stories behind most of them. At this point my blood was flowing and I could feel my heart pounding—and then it hit me: it wasn't my heart. I stopped dead in my tracks at the thought. Some kid died and I got his heart; now my heart was in a garbage can somewhere, and his heart was beating in my chest.

As the wind whistled through the trees, I heard *Not my heart, not my heart, not my heart* going through my mind in time with the pounding heartbeat. I shook myself, trying to rid it of the thought, and then took two deep breaths and started to run again.

The park path went through the woods and ended by the school's athletic fields and playground. I saw little kids on the swings and others running around throwing mulch at each other. A girl was inside the soccer goal and another was taking shots—they could have been Becca and me five years ago. I stood and watched them for a few minutes as I jogged in place.

"Emmi," someone shouted and I turned around. It was Eric, Becca's prom date. I hadn't seen him since the prom.

"Hey," he said. "You're running! That's great."

"It's my first time running and it feels good," I said, running in place. "How's your summer been?" I asked him. He gave me a strange look and I couldn't help wondering if it was because of my moon face. Well, at least he recognized me.

"Summer's good. Better for you, too, now that Sam's done with camp, right?"

"He's done with camp?" I said, clearly surprised. How could he not tell me? Hadn't I asked?

"Um, yeah," he said, clearly uncomfortable. "I thought you knew."

"Oh, I knew, I just lost track of the days," I told him. "They all seem to blend." Eric was a good guy and I didn't want him to feel bad, but I had to get out of there. "I'm going to keep running, Eric. See you around."

"Yeah, Emmi. See you later," he said.

I turned around and ran back to the path through the woods. Wow, was I so out of touch with my boyfriend that I didn't know he was done with his summer job? What had happened to us?

Yes, I'd been totally wrapped up in recovering and trying to get back in shape and everything, but I couldn't believe we'd drifted this far apart. I was shocked by this bit of news—which I had to hear from Eric—and I didn't even know what I'd say to Sam about it, the next time we even talked.

46

"Bec, I ran today," I said as soon as she answered her cell. "I did four whole miles!"

"That's great, Emmi," she said.

"I met up with Eric today on my run. Did you know Sam was done with camp?"

"I haven't talked to Sam," she said.

"Why wouldn't Sam have told me? Don't you think that's kind of odd? He's been acting kind of weird lately—do you think something's wrong?" But she was silent. "Bec, are you there?"

"Yeah, I'm here."

"What's happening, Bec? You're my best friend—tell me the truth: what do you think's going on?"

"I'm sure it's nothing," she said, but her voice told me something different.

"Bec, I know you—something else is up and you have to tell me if you know."

"I'm sure it's nothing," she said.

"It's sounding like it's something—I can tell by your voice," I answered.

"Listen, Em. Can I come over, or is your mom still being a total Nazi?"

"She's still being careful, but, yeah, you can come over. I sure would love the company—my parents are out and Eli's at Tommy's. Jeremy's here, but a zombie-baseball fan watching his beloved Yankees doesn't count."

"There's something I have to tell you." Then she hung up. *Something she has to tell me? What can it be? Is it about Sam? Is he cheating on me? Is it about Becca? Is she sick? Pregnant? She swore she didn't have sex at Duke, but who knows?*

How was I supposed to get through the next five minutes until she came over and spilled whatever it was?

I went downstairs and got some water, then went through the cabinets looking for something to eat. I wasn't really hungry, but I needed something to do until Becca showed up.

Jeremy was lying on the couch watching the Yankee game in the family room and I sat down with him.

"Who's winning?" I asked.

"What do you care?" he said, his eyes not moving from the screen. "You *hate* baseball."

"I do care. Who's winning?"

"Yankees, 6-3."

"Jeremy, have I changed since the transplant?" That got his attention and he sat up and looked at me.

"In what way?" he asked.

"I don't know. Does my personality seem different?"

"No, you're still bossy. Why do you ask?"

"Sam and Becca have been weird around me lately, and Sam hardly ever comes over anymore."

"Maybe if he can't kiss you and stuff, it's not worth it to him. Or maybe it's too hard to sit next to you, knowing you can't do anything . . . like that." Then he pretend fainted.

"Will you stop with the melodrama? Do you really think that's it?"

"Probably can't get past the moon face," he said. Brothers are so obnoxious sometimes.

Then the doorbell rang and I stuck my head out the door. "Meet me around back," I said to Becca, then ran through the house—without getting winded—to the patio.

"It's amazing to see you—you look so tan," I said. But she wasn't smiling. This must be really bad.

"It's good to see you, too," she said. "How're you feeling?"

"So much better. I can do everything now! It felt awesome to run today."

"That's great," she said. But her voice was flat and she showed no enthusiasm—not the kind of reaction I expected at all, not from my BFF.

"Bec, what's going on?" She looked like she was about to give me the worst news of my life. Then I thought I had it: "Oh, my God, am I off the team? After all this? Please don't tell me that's it—I really couldn't handle it after everything I've been through."

"It's got nothing to do with soccer," Becca said, and then she took a deep breath and went on. "You remember the night Sam and I came to visit you in the ICU?"

"Vaguely. I kind of remember you guys being there and Sam getting upset about something. I was in and out of it."

"Sam gave you a hard time about your friend Abe."

"But we're just friends."

"Sam knew that. But he was freaked out about the transplant and you almost dying and everything, and then he felt guilty he was giving you a hard time when you'd just been through all that."

"Is that why he didn't come back to the hospital?" I asked.

"Partly."

"All right—just tell me what's going on."

"He was really down when we were walking out of the hospital so we talked for a while, then left for home in our cars. But then my cell rang and it was Sam. One of his friends was having a party and he wanted me to go with him. He wasn't in a partying mood, but he thought it might make him feel better. He wanted me along because I was the only one who knew what he was going through."

"So you went?" I wasn't sure where this was going, but it didn't sound good.

"I was exhausted; remember, I hadn't been home from camp yet. I'd driven straight from camp to the hospital. I told him I needed to go home and change, and would meet him there."

"Did you go?"

"I almost didn't—I was so wiped out. But I felt bad because I knew how bummed he was about everything.

Anyway, by the time I got there, he was trashed. Someone handed me a drink and Sam and I started talking. He felt so guilty about leaving the hospital after giving you a hard time about Abe. And I was dead tired, physically and emotionally, and I decided I wanted to get wasted, too. I don't know who was in charge of refills, but somebody kept my glass full.

"Before I knew it, I was drunk. Some guy came and dragged me over to where people were dancing. We were having fun but then I noticed Sam sitting off to the side, looking sad. I went over and tried to get him to dance, to get him out of his funk. He didn't want to but I finally got him dancing with me. We were so wasted we were tripping over each other's feet." She scrunched her face from the memory of it all, and I was at the edge of my seat, knowing somehow that this would get worse before she was done.

"Keep going, Bec," I said. "I don't like where this is going. Did you get home?"

"This is the bad part, Em," she said. "A slow song came on and we were crying in each other's arms."

"And then?"

"And then I kissed him."

"You kissed Sam?" I cried.

"I slept with Sam, Emmi."

If she'd kicked me in the chest and recracked my sternum it would have hurt less than this. Tears clouded my eyes and I felt a panic come over me.

"Becca, please go."

"We didn't mean for it to happen," she said.

"But it did."

"Only once."

"That was one time too many. Now please, just leave."
I turned and ran into the house, past Jeremy, up the stairs, and into my room. I threw myself on the bed, sobbing deep sobs, the kind that don't let you catch your breath between them. I heard footsteps in the hallway and they came into my room.

"Emmi, please forgive me. I'm so sorry," Becca said.

"GET THE HELL OUT," I screamed. "There's nothing you can say that makes this okay. *Nothing!*"

"We were both upset about you, and about everything that'd been happening to you after the transplant."

"So you had sex with each other? Oh yeah, I can see how that helped."

"No—you don't see. And it *was* wrong, but you don't know how hard everything was for us through all these months. You were only thinking about yourself and what you were going through, but it was hard for *us*, too."

She was crying now, but she couldn't be feeling nearly as bad as I was.

"So now it's my fault you two slept together? Are you kidding me?"

"No, I'm not saying it's your fault," she said. "But it just happened. We were drunk and it was wrong, and I'm so, so sorry, Emmi."

"That's such bullshit. Get out of my room and get out of my house—NOW!"

She walked out and I slammed the bedroom door after

her. I kicked my soccer ball into the wall a few times. Then I saw the collage of us from when we were nine years old. I yanked it off the wall and shattered it over the back of my desk chair. Pieces of glass flew everywhere and my hand was bleeding, but I didn't care.

How could my two best friends betray me like that? And pretty unbelievable coming from the queen of the "no sex" pact. Now I understand why they both seemed to be avoiding me—they were!

I was more angry than sad now, and I felt the sudden need to confront Sam. I was sure Becca was telling the truth, but I had to hear it from him directly. I dialed his cell number knowing Becca had probably given him a heads-up. I was sure he wouldn't even answer it. And just as I expected, it rang and rang. The coward—he couldn't even talk to me.

And then I heard his voice saying hello.

Overwhelmed, I started crying and hung up. *Oh, God, I loved him so much and he did this to me.*

My cell rang and it was Sam. I didn't know if I should pick it up, but I did want to hear what he had to say. I let him suffer through four long rings, then summoned my perkiest, tear-free voice: "Hello?"

"Emmi, it's me. I know you spoke to Becca and I'm coming over."

"You've barely been here in the past month, and *now* you're coming over?"

"We need to talk."

"Do we?" I asked.

"Yes, we do. I'll be there in five minutes." He hung up.

I rushed into the bathroom and splashed cold water on my face; my nose was still bright red from crying, and I washed the cut on my hand and looked for a Band-Aid. All I found was a Scooby-Doo one, but that was good enough.

Walking downstairs, I had no idea what I was going to say. *Should I hear him out? Tell him off?* I didn't think there was anything that could excuse this. *My boyfriend and my best friend? Is anything ever going to be the same in my life?*

Jeremy hadn't moved from his position on the family room couch, but he looked up as I walked through the room.

"You okay?"

"Fine," I said, which seemed to satisfy him.

I went outside and sat on the front steps and waited. Sam's car pulled up and he got out, slamming the door. He walked slowly to the steps and we stared at each other. I was so angry, but seeing him, I felt myself crumbling.

"How could you do that to me—," I started.

"I'm so sorry—," he said at the same time.

"It doesn't make any sense," I said as he sat down next to me. "My best friend and my boyfriend—the two people I trusted most in the world. I've got nothing now."

"It was a drunken mistake."

"Alcohol is a bullshit excuse, Sam. Have you always been attracted to her? Or was she a lousy substitute because you couldn't have me?"

"You're analyzing it way too much."

"Then tell me why it happened!"

"I don't know why. I've been trying to figure it out for the past six weeks."

"I hate you both," I said.

"You know what, Em, we've all been through a lot."

"This is *not* as hard on you as it's been on me."

"But it hasn't been easy," Sam said. "I'm seventeen years old and my girlfriend almost died. I'm sorry if I'm not perfect and didn't deal with it in the most perfect way. I think I've been pretty damn supportive all these months."

"You were supportive, Sam. You were amazing— almost too amazing. I guess I should've known it couldn't be real."

"It *is* so real. I'm here, aren't I?"

"Then why didn't you tell me?"

"*This* is why. Because I didn't want to lose you."

"But I knew there was something not right between us. I knew things weren't normal and blamed myself, sure it was something I did. I had no idea it was something *you* did. And you were such a coward! You waited until Becca told me first, so you didn't have to do it yourself."

"She shouldn't have told you," he said.

"Yes, she should have. And you should have—six weeks ago, instead of abandoning me all this time, letting me wonder what *I'd* done wrong."

Then, as if on cue, Becca's car pulled up.

"Nobody wants to see me for weeks and now everyone wants to see me?" Becca ran to us, her eyes were all red and puffy. Good—*she should suffer, too.* "Well, if it isn't the boyfriend-stealing slut."

"That's not fair!" she said.

"It's totally fair," I replied. "Why'd you come back? Did you come to get Sam?"

"There's nothing between us," they said in unison.

"Then *what the hell happened*?"

Looking at both of them standing there, I started picturing them together: her kissing him and him touching her; oh, God, it was awful. I couldn't take it anymore—I had to get away from them. I walked away, around the house to the backyard, my head spinning. I didn't know which of them I hated more.

I sat down on the porch swing and started rocking. I thought about all the nights Sam and I had sat in this swing, talking about everything from the future to books to sports to—everything. And I pictured nine-year-old Becca and me playing in my backyard for hours. One summer we set up a fort in the back of the bushes and ate lunch there almost every day. *How could the two best people in my life do this to me? And how can I lose them both at the same time?* I hugged my knees to my chin and kept rocking.

There were footsteps on the patio but I didn't want to look up. I had nothing else to say to either Becca or Sam.

"Em?" It was Jeremy.

"Yeah?"

"What's going on? You're out here and Sam and Becca are on the front lawn."

"Is the game over?" I asked.

"How'd you know?"

"Because you tuned back in," I said. "I can't believe they're still there."

"What happened?" he asked.

"You're too young—I can't explain this to you," I told him.

But he sat down next to me anyway. "Not really, Em. Seventh grade can teach you a lot of things."

"They did something really stupid."

"Did they do the nasty?" he asked.

"Nasty's probably the right word for it."

"Did you and Sam ever—?"

"None of your business," I said, then added, "No."

"But he did it with her? I don't get it."

"Me neither. They're really still there?"

"Yeah. And now I may have to beat the crap out of him," Jeremy said, getting up out of the swing.

"That's sweet, bro, but I don't think it's necessary." I stood up. "I know I need to go back out there and face them, but I don't know what I want to do, how I want this to go."

"Do you love him?" Jeremy asked. Wow, was this really my obnoxious little brother talking?

"I do, Jem. But this is just so huge."

"Gandhi once said, 'The weak can never forgive. Forgiveness is the attribute of the strong.' "

"Who are you and what have you done with my younger brother?" I asked, staring at him in amazement.

"I'm not just about baseball, Em. Besides, Dad and I watched a show on him the other day."

"Who knew?" I hugged my brother, who wasn't as little as I thought, and started to walk to the front of the house. I went slowly and tried to organize my thoughts: was I weak or strong?

As I turned the corner, I watched Sam and Becca standing there, looking so awkward together. Maybe they were right and it *was* just a one-night thing. But it still happened and nothing would ever change that. How could I get past it? How could I trust either of them again?

I had a new heart beating in my chest; maybe it was time to start fresh and move on. No point having a pity party, as my mom said.

As I walked toward them, I suddenly turned around, as if my body knew better what to do than I did, and that I just wasn't ready. I went in the back door and up to my room, crawling into bed and curling up with my pillow. That's when the enormity of it all hit me again: two days after I got my transplant, when I was fighting for my life, my best friend and my boyfriend slept together.

I got up and peeked out the window. They were still there, leaning against Sam's car, not speaking or even looking at each other. I truly hoped they were hurting as much as I was. Then Sam looked up at the window and saw me watching them. I jumped away from the window.

"Emmi!" Sam shouted and I closed the window.

A few seconds later, the doorbell rang and Sam started pounding on the door. I went to the top of the steps where I could see the door, but I didn't make a move to open it.

"Emmi, please. Can we talk?" Sam shouted through the door.

"Emmi! Come on, talk to us," Becca shouted.

I hoped my parents weren't going to come home in the middle of all of this—it wouldn't be pretty.

Then Jeremy came into the hallway and looked at me. "What are you going to do?"

I shrugged. "Nothing right now," I said and went back to my bedroom.

Sam knocked one more time, and a few minutes later I heard his car start and he left. Then Becca went, too; maybe they were going to have sympathy sex again. I didn't even care.

No, that was a lie. I *totally* cared.

47

Both Sam and Becca tried calling me a dozen times that week but I ignored them. If I saw it was one of them on my caller ID, I just didn't pick up. If I was online and I saw them log on, I immediately logged off. And once, when Eli answered the phone, I refused to take Sam's call. *Let them both suffer.*

But they weren't the only ones suffering; my loneliness reached its all-time low. I read a book once about a girl who had cancer. As she got sicker, her friends didn't know how to deal with her and her parents couldn't comfort her. That's when she realized people are all alone. Once she accepted this, she found new strength. Maybe that was the approach I needed to take: confidence and strength in being alone.

Who was I kidding? I was a sixteen-year-old, extremely social being. And I was terrible at being alone. I'd gotten accustomed to isolation from everything I'd been through, but the truth was, I needed people, especially my closest ones. I logged on to the computer looking for some human contact. And as usual on this beautiful summer day, no one I knew was online; my friends were all the outdoors type, and there's no way they'd be cooped up inside with their computers on a day like today.

I wanted to be able to talk to someone about what'd happened with Sam and Becca, but the two people I usually told everything were Sam and Becca. Lauren was in Europe, but I thought about calling Noelle; did she know? I loved Noelle, but she wasn't really my go-to girl when it came to problems. Abe and I texted or talked all the time, but I couldn't tell him about this. We spent hours discussing books and all the music he loved; and we debated silly things, like the best combination of ice cream flavors in a hot fudge sundae. But I never mentioned Sam. It was like I wanted to reserve Abe in a separate, private corner of my life, away from all the other people. When I was talking to Abe I wasn't thinking about Sam and Becca, or lamenting everything I'd given up in the past year, or even worrying about all the scary possibilities of the future. With Abe, I just enjoyed a good time with my good new friend.

At least running and my training with Eli kept me busy. One Saturday morning, even my mom tried to join me for a run. She was an excellent speed-walker, but not a great runner; she gave up less than a mile into the park, and we walked briskly for the rest of the path. At the three-mile mark we took a break and sat down on one of the benches, which was nothing more than large strips of jagged wood nailed together.

"Think we'll get splinters?" my mother asked.

"Nah. But don't let your legs touch the wood," I said. We both sat there with only the edges of our backsides touching the bench as we drank water and rested for a while.

"How are you?" Mom asked.

"I'm good. I've been running this path every day, so the walk is easy for me."

"That's not what I meant."

Does she know about Sam and Becca? I hadn't told my parents, but I was being mopier than usual. I'd decided not to say anything to them about it; I wasn't in the mood for their "when I was your age" attempts at comfort.

"What do you mean?" She might be trying to get it out of me, but I was going to make her work for it.

"Jeremy told me." She wasn't going to work for it—it was right there, out in the open now and we were going straight to it.

I shrugged and stood up, stretching my legs and getting ready to walk again. "Are you ready to keep going?" I asked.

"Emmi, talk to me. You must be so hurt."

"No, I'm fine. Let's just walk, okay?"

But after a whole week of holding everything inside, here was someone willing to listen and I just couldn't do it—I couldn't talk about it. I started walking again and she had no choice but to come along.

"So when's Dad coming home today?"

"He had a client who needed something, but he should be home soon." We walked the rest of the way back to the house without speaking. It was a humid day, and by the time we got home our shirts were soaking wet. Taking my pulse felt great—my new heart was going strong and fast.

As we were walking across the grass, my father pulled into the driveway with someone in his passenger seat.

"I didn't know we were having company," I said.

She smiled. "Go over and say hi," she urged.

"Who is it?" I said as I walked over to my dad's car. Then the passenger door opened and Abe got out.

"Abe!" I shouted, overjoyed. "Omigod, I'm such a mess!" I said, looking down at my sweatiness. My hair was in a ponytail, but one piece kept falling in my eyes; I swiped it up and it was so wet that it stuck to my head. "I can't even hug you—I'm way too gross."

He looked at me and laughed. "Yeah, you truly are," he agreed. My heart was beating a little faster and I could feel my face turning red. It could have been from the walk, but I knew it was probably from seeing Abe.

I looked at him and couldn't stop smiling; it was so great to see him.

"Good run?" my father asked, getting out of the car.

"We found out Mom's not a runner," I said, "but it was a good walk." Dad laughed. "Were you really working, or did you go into the city just to get Abe?"

"A little bit of both. I got a few hours of work in before I went uptown to pick up Abe."

"This is such a great surprise! Let me take a shower and I'll be down in five minutes," I said to Abe. "Meanwhile, come on in."

239

Abe opened the back door of the car and pulled out two giant shopping bags.

"What'd you bring?" I asked, trying to look in the bags.

"Go—I'll show you when you're all cleaned up."

48

After the world's fastest shower, I towel-dried my hair and got dressed, throwing on a tank top and shorts, then put on some makeup and pulled my hair back in a ponytail again. I couldn't believe Abe had come to see me, and that my parents knew about it and didn't tell me. What a great surprise—and such a great distraction from the whole Sam and Becca mess. I dashed down the stairs two at a time, then went into the kitchen to find Abe talking with my dad. Yes, they were talking about music; amazing that my father and my friend Abe liked the same stuff.

"Two friends and I have a music blog," Abe told my father. "You should check it out."

"What's it called?" Dad asked.

"Oldguysrockpicks.com," Abe answered. Dad and I looked at each other.

"Old guys?" I asked.

"It's written by me, Leo, and Morty, so we thought since we all have old-guy names it might work."

"Abe, Leo, and Morty?" I asked. "Do the kids at school

give you a lot of grief for that?" What happened to Abe not having any friends?

"Well, Morty is John Mortinson and he's captain of the football team, so they back off."

"You *are not* best friends with the captain of the football team," I said, laughing.

"Why is that so hard to believe?" he asked. "Okay, I confess—it's a really small school and most of these kids have IQs off the charts, so Morty's also on the math team and probably not your typical captain of the football team, but still."

"Do you play on the team?" Dad asked.

"They're not that desperate," he said, laughing.

"So what'd you bring me?" I asked.

"Nice to see you, too," he said.

"I'm going to try to make some headway on the gardening. I'll see you guys later," my dad said, leaving the room.

I grabbed the first bag and started looking through it, pulling out a heavy glossy magazine. "*Calcio Italia*—my favorite Italian soccer magazine! We read it when we were in Italy. Omigod, Abe! Where did you find this?"

"The guy that owns the newsstand on our corner is from Italy. He said they weren't available on newsstands here anymore, but he had a cousin with a subscription," Abe explained. "And for a small price, that cousin was willing to part with this month's copy."

"This is totally amazing." I started flipping through it. "I know so many of these guys!"

"It's all in Italian," Abe said.

"Doesn't matter. It's fun to look at the pictures. I just love those soccer bodies."

"Hey!" Abe protested.

"If you're going to be my friend, you have to know I've got a weakness for them," I teased.

"I didn't know Sam was a soccer player," he said and I blushed. I still hadn't told Abe anything about what had happened.

"Okay, I made an exception," I said. "What else do you have for me?" I had to get the conversation away from Sam.

"Well, I know there're two sides to you, so while I was visiting the Italian newsstand guy, he suggested I give you this, too." He pulled out a copy of *Vogue Italian.*

"Wow, Abe. Thank you! Now I have something great to do tomorrow."

"Here's the thing: I knew you were bored out of your mind, and I remembered how a few weeks after my transplant I was climbing the walls from boredom, too. And I didn't have a backyard to go to. I sat in that apartment for almost two months after my transplant."

"Kind of like this summer was for you," I said.

"Nah, I was just messing with you—I went out a lot this summer. But I figured that the last thing you needed to hear about was my booming social life."

"From everything you've told me, the only thing booming was your iPod."

"Maybe the truth's somewhere in the middle," he conceded. "I wasn't home all day—and I did go out here and there."

I smiled at him and our eyes met.

"It's so nice to be with someone who understands what I'm going through. Thank you so much for coming today, Abe." I took his hand and we sat for a minute, looking at each other, smiling and holding hands. Was something happening between us? It felt like it, but I was still unsettled about everything with Sam.

Do I want something to happen with my friend Abe? Does Abe even think about me that way? And what about Sam? I hated to admit it, but I still loved him—at least I thought I did. And if I did, then why was I so elated to be sitting here with Abe?

Abe looked away and started fishing through the bag, this time pulling out a giant hardcover book.

"*The Rolling Stone Encyclopedia of Rock and Roll*," Abe said. "It's the bible."

I took the book from him and flipped through it. "Wow—eleven hundred and thirty-six pages—that's something to do in my spare time."

"All your time is spare time these days from what I hear."

"Thanks for pointing that out," I said, laughing. It was such fun to be with Abe—and so easy.

"There *will* be a test on this book at the end of the month."

"Yes, teacher." I lifted the book over my head—it was heavy. "I can always use it for weight training."

"Have some respect for the bible," Abe said.

I got up and laid the book on the table and bowed to it. He laughed.

"That's a big bag. What else do you have in there?"

"Well, it's been proven that chocolate's a mood elevator," he said as he pulled out a giant box of chocolates. "This should keep you in a good mood for a while."

"I'm in a good mood *now*, but let's have one anyway," I said as I opened the box. "Want one?"

"I'm in a good mood, too, but sure, you can twist my arm."

We sat there enjoying the chocolates. And of course we couldn't eat only one, so we each had a few more. Our moods were going to be off the charts pretty soon.

"And now, for the greatest gift of all," Abe said, standing up and reaching into the bag.

"I'm not sure you're going to top the chocolates," I said, my mouth full.

"Oh, yeah. I think I can," he said, pulling out a deck of cards.

"A deck of cards? That's the grand finale, the big gift? Um, thanks."

"First of all, you can get hours of enjoyment out of a simple deck of cards. I, myself, am the master of solitaire."

"Okay, enough about your love life," I said.

"Low blow."

"Sorry."

"True, but low blow nevertheless."

"Have you ever had a girlfriend?" I asked.

"Nah. The girls in my school are too—"

"Snobby?"

"It's not that; it's—"

"Too shallow?"

"No—it's kind of the opposite. They're way too impressed with themselves."

"Yeah, I know what you mean. We've got a bunch of girls like that at my school, too."

"And besides, all the good ones are taken," he said, looking into my eyes.

He looked so cute sitting there. There was only one thing to do: change the subject.

"So what's the deal about these cards?" I asked.

"I'm going to teach you to play poker," Abe said.

"If you say the word 'strip' I'll hit you. I wondered how long it would be until you started taking your shirt off again!"

He started shuffling the cards and was as good as a dealer in a casino. "No, I'm keeping it clean," he said. "You'll be learning from the master."

"Wow—a master at solitaire *and* a master at poker. You're pretty masterful."

"My grandfather Abe was a professional card player," Abe said, shuffling the cards again. "He taught my mom, and she taught me."

"I didn't realize it was the family business," I said.

Abe dealt us each five cards, saying, "Watch and learn."

We played poker for hours. He taught me strategy and how to bluff; my brothers came home and he taught them to play, too. We used dried kidney beans for money, and by the end of the day I had the biggest pile of beans of all.

Later that night, Dad and I drove Abe back into the city. It'd been a fabulous day; he cared enough about me to find all of those things to bring me. And he understood me—what a great guy.

49

That week I kept busy with running and enjoying all the things Abe had brought me. I still thought about Sam constantly, but the pain was dulling a little.

I picked up the phone to call Becca a few times, but I couldn't go through with it. Eventually she stopped calling me but I couldn't imagine our friendship was over. But I totally needed the space.

My brothers, meanwhile, were willing poker opponents. August was a quiet time for soccer and baseball, so we started a nightly poker game at the table on our patio. Sometimes even my parents would join us.

"Let's go to Twist and Shake for some ice cream," my dad suggested one night after winning a big poker hand.

"If you'd let us play for money instead of beans, I'd have enough to treat the whole family," I said. I was enjoying poker and getting good at it; I couldn't wait to play Abe again and see if I could take down "the master."

My brothers didn't need to be asked twice to go for ice cream and they ran inside to get their sneakers.

Twist and Shake was one of our favorite summer places; it was basically a big shack with windows. People drove up and walked over to the window to order their ice cream, and they served giant soft-serve cones. On a hot day it was a race to lick the ice cream before it melted and dripped down your arm. And it being an outdoor place made it okay with my germ-phobic mother.

"I just need a few minutes to get ready," I said and dashed upstairs. With the exception of my daily run through the park, I hadn't been seen in public for a while. Since you never knew who you would bump into at Twist and Shake, and we usually saw at least a few people we knew on any given night, I wanted to be presentable. I looked in the mirror; there wasn't much I could do about the moon face, but I put on mascara, blush, and some lip gloss and went down to find my family already in the van.

We pulled into Twist and Shake and found a spot right in front. There were about ten people on each line—average for a summer night. I was nervous about running into anyone I knew, but part of me kind of hoped I'd see someone—I missed being around people. We all hopped out of the car and got on the shorter line.

Then Jeremy said, "Emmi, look," pointing to the front of the right line.

It was Sam. What were the odds?

"Are you going to say hi?" my brother asked.

At first, all I could think of was whether I could make it back to the car without him seeing me. But did I really want to? And who was he with? Was he there with a girl? I knew I couldn't handle that.

I looked again and saw Eric and another guy from the baseball team—Steven? Sam was wearing gym shorts and a tank top, and the view from behind was both awesome and painful at the same time. I watched him for a few minutes and so many memories came flooding back.

I still had time to escape, but I didn't try. Instead I walked over and tapped him on the shoulder.

He turned around and maybe I wanted to see this, but it looked like his eyes sparkled with pleasure.

"Hi," I said, nervously making eye contact.

"Hi," he said. He seemed nervous, too, and surprised. But happy, too, I think. "Who are you here with?" he asked.

"My parents and my brothers."

"Let me go say hi to the boys," he said.

"No. Let's go talk first," I said, taking his hand. "Oh, you didn't get your ice cream."

"It can wait. Guys, I'll be back," he said to Eric and Steven.

Then we walked behind the shack and sat side by side at one of the empty picnic tables set up for people to eat their ice cream.

"How are you feeling?" he asked me.

"I'm good—really good so far." We sat there in silence for a minute, looking at each other, but both hesitant.

"School's starting soon," I said.

"Yeah. Senior year—should be good."

"I'm not starting right away. Dr. Leavens said I can go back on October first."

"That's not so bad."

We were talking, but it was awkward and we both looked down at the ground. Sam kicked a rock away and I traced the dirt with my sandal.

"What can I say to make this better?" Sam asked me.

"Nothing, Sam. It happened and I hate you," I said, looking into his amazing eyes. Then I sighed. "But I love you, too."

"I love you, too, Emmi." He leaned over to kiss me.

But I held up my hand to stop him. "Not yet," I said. "I'm sorry—but soon."

"This is so impossible! I so want to kiss you."

I ran my fingers through his hair; it'd gotten lighter in the sun.

"I just keep wanting to ask you *why*?" I finally said.

"There's still no good answer to that," he said.

"But how can I be with you without thinking about it?" I asked, looking up to see him gazing directly at me.

"I don't know, Emmi," he said. "Maybe you can't."

We sat there in silence for a minute.

"So, are you taking honors English again?" I asked, steering him toward a neutral topic.

"Yeah. You?"

"Yeah. They told me I should take regular classes since I was starting late, but I figured if I could keep up last year, after being sick and missing half the school year, just missing a month wouldn't be a big deal."

"I'll help you," he offered.

"But no messing around while we study," I warned.

"That was the best part," he said, laughing.

"Yeah, it was," I said, looking into his eyes. "Let's go get some ice cream."

We held hands and walked back to the line, joining my parents and brothers. My mom looked at me, nodded, and smiled. Eli jumped on Sam and he gave Eli a high five.

Then Sam took my hand again and we stood waiting for our ice cream. I leaned against him and he put his arm around me. It was nice to be back together.

Now I had to find Becca.

50

Sam left with his friends and I came home with my parents. I thanked them for the ice cream and went upstairs; and as usual, I went to see who was on the computer. Becca's name was up and I sat for a minute in front of the computer, trying to think of what to say when she chatted me.

Becca: *Hey. u didn't log off. R u there?*

Emmi: *I'm here. Sup?*

Becca: *nm u?*

Emmi: *Went to Twist N Shake.*

Becca: *o*

Emmi: *Saw Sam.*

Becca: *o*

Emmi: *I'm still pissed at u guys. But I've missed u, 2. I can't believe u did that 2 me.*

Becca: *I wish I could take it back. Turn back time and fix it.*

Emmi: *But u can't.*

Becca: *No, I can't.*

Emmi: *Jeremy told me that Gandhi said that the strong can forgive. I'm not so sure I'm the strong.*

Becca: *Jeremy's quoting Gandhi?*

Emmi: *I know. Hard 2 believe. But he didn't want me 2 lose u.*

Becca: *u didn't lose me. I'm still here.*

Emmi: *Good. Can u come over 2morrow?*

Becca: *I had plans but I'll cancel them. Let's hang out.*

Emmi: *k. Call me in the morning. Night.*

Becca: *ttyl, my friend.*

51

The rest of the summer passed quietly; Sam and Becca came by often and we fell back into our old easiness together. I'd never forget what happened, but as time went on the anger softened.

Meanwhile, I kept running and Eli had me doing drills. Dad tried not to push me too much, but I could tell he was hoping I'd return to soccer strong. Dr. Leavens said if I was feeling good and there were no health concerns, I could start practicing with my team on October first, the same day I went back to school. I'd have preferred September first, but I wasn't going to argue about an extra month after being out all this time already.

Weekly biopsies and doctor's appointments were big activities, and so far no rejection; but you were never out of the woods with a transplant—not ever. But with each biopsy I crossed my fingers and prayed a little; I'd become a model pill taker and wasn't even late by a minute.

Abe kept me laughing with his daily chatting; he was also my anchor and role model when it came to my heart transplant. I couldn't have gotten through it without his encouragement, and even though I loved Sam, I also had a bit of a crush on Abe.

I came in after a run one day and turned on my computer. One second later, Abe requested a video chat.

"Where've you been?" Abe asked.

"Out running," I said. "As you can see by the sweat pouring down my face and the running clothes I'm wearing. Don't you have anything to do all day besides wait by the computer for me to get home?"

"Down, girl," he said. "Actually, Leo and Morty are here, and we're figuring out what to post on our first-anniversary blog."

"Why are you talking to me if your friends are there?" I asked. "Hi, Leo. Hi, Morty." I heard mumbling from Abe's side.

"We took a break. Leo wants to do a vlog with video, and Morty's too busy texting his girlfriend to pay attention to us."

"Does Leo know a lot about video?" I asked. Dad had started talking about my video reel for the college coaches.

"Yeah, he's starting a TV thing at school, which is kinda stupid considering there aren't even a hundred kids in the whole school. Who's going to watch it?"

"I'm putting it online," I heard Leo shout from the background. "It's going to go viral."

"He's got big dreams," Abe said.

"Big dreams are good," I said. Were we allowed big dreams when every biopsy brought uncertainty? Was Abe thinking that, too? My cell vibrated and I saw it was a text from Sam. It would wait. "I may need his editing help."

"Something good?" Abe asked.

"Just a little soccer thing, maybe," I said. There was a scuffle behind Abe.

"Give me my cell phone, you dork," Morty screamed.

"Hey, loverboy, can we focus on the blog?" Leo said. "Log off."

The screen went blank. I watched it for another minute to see if he'd come back, then walked away, disappointed. My cell vibrated again and I ignored it, heading for the shower.

The next night I was on Facebook when Abe started a chat.

Abe:	*Hey, Emmi. 'sup?*
Emmi:	*nm u?*
Abe:	*Got back from my mother's coworker's beach club.*
Emmi:	*Fun?*
Abe:	*Boring. My mom and her friend brought work with them and I sat there doing Sudoko and reading comic books the whole time.*
Emmi:	*And playing solitaire, oh master?*
Abe:	*All by myself.*
Emmi:	*There was no 1 ur age?*
Abe:	*Yeah, but they were jerks.*
Emmi:	*o*
Abe:	*And it sucks to have people always asking about my scar.*

Emmi:	*I thought about that myself. So much for looking great in a bikini.*
Abe:	*I'm sure you'll still look great.*
Emmi:	*Yeah, with the big moon face and the exclamation point scar, I'm going 2 B the hit of the beach next summer.*
Abe:	*U R 2 hard on yourself.*
Emmi:	*Nah. Just realistic.*
Abe:	*Stop. I'm the King of self-deprecation and I will let you b my Queen.*
Emmi:	*You'd b lucky to have me as your Queen.*
Abe:	*Quite right, m'lady. But alas, it's not meant 2 B.*

What do I answer to that? And is it meant to be?

I needed to think of something clever to say back—quickly. But my mind was a blank so I did something stupid—I logged off. It's the Facebook equivalent of hanging up on someone.

How could I do that to him? What was I thinking? I didn't even say "g2g" or "bi bi" or anything that would have passed for polite.

I paced my bedroom for several minutes and kicked the soccer ball against the wall, trying to figure out what to do. If I logged on again, I had to come up with some good excuse for getting off so abruptly. If I didn't log on again, how would I face him next time?

I had to apologize—or lie. That's it! I'd say that Eli came in and started goofing around and accidentally logged me off. That was believable—I'd often told Abe what a pest Eli could be. He'd always respond with "You're lucky to have a brother," which I guess I was, although I didn't always feel that way.

I went back into Facebook intending to lie about logging off so abruptly like that. Except Abe wasn't online.

People my age are never more than a gadget away from each other, so I tried to call him on his cell: no answer. This was odd because he always had his cell with him—Jane insisted, saying it made her feel better knowing she could reach him at any time.

Is he avoiding me? Over something so silly that easily could have been caused by my pain-in-the-neck brother? It wasn't, but it could have been.

After ten minutes of pacing and ball kicking, I tried his cell again. This time I left a message with the whole lame excuse. Then I pushed End and tossed the stupid phone on my bed.

What have I done?

52

How many times can you try someone's cell phone without looking pathetic?

I e-mailed Abe and kept logging on to the computer to see if I could catch him, but I'd come to the conclusion he was avoiding me and it hurt—a lot. What they say is true; we don't appreciate what we have until it's gone. I even listened to hours of Abe's music in the strange hope it'd put us in sync and he'd call me back.

Sam came over a few nights later and we sat together on the porch swing, rocking. Sam was sitting up and I was curled up in his lap. He was talking nervously about the upcoming school year; I was listening to him, but I wasn't hearing him at all. I was too caught up in how to apologize to Abe.

"I can't stay late," he said. "Even senior year, my mom wants me in bed early before the first day of school."

"Yeah," I said, absentmindedly.

"Emmi, are you there?"

I sat up. "Of course. What do you mean?"

"You haven't been very enthusiastic tonight—it's like you're somewhere else. *Are* you somewhere else?"

Time to come up with something—and it had to be better than "I've been worried about my friendship with Abe all night." Sam had made it clear that he didn't appreciate it when so many of my sentences started with "Abe said." But it wasn't my fault that Abe was the only person I had to guide me through all this post-transplant stuff. It wasn't like Sam got angry before the transplant, when most of my sentences started with "Dr. Leavens said." But I guess this *was* kind of different, since Abe was a guy my age.

"It's hard to hear all about school when I still have another month before I can go back," I said. Excellent—this was the perfect excuse! It was reasonable and wouldn't arouse suspicion.

Evidently Sam thought it was good, too, as he leaned over and put the sweetest kiss on my cheek.

"I'm sorry," he said. "I wasn't thinking." Then I turned to face him and looking into those awesome eyes made me forget about Abe for a while. I wanted to kiss Sam so badly and it took every bit of my strength to pull away.

"How much longer?" he moaned.

"It's almost nine weeks since the surgery," I said. "I'll talk to Dr. Leavens at my appointment next week." For the past eight weeks, the doctor visits and biopsies had been weekly, but now I was up to every other week and it felt like a vacation.

"And do you think we could get permission for . . . other things?" he asked, looking into my eyes. That made a shiver go through my whole body.

"The pact with Becca seems a little, well, over," I said.

He didn't look at me—it was the first direct reference either of us had made to the Becca-Sam mess in the past few weeks. I curled up in his lap again and kissed the side of his neck.

"Don't torture me," he said.

What could one kiss hurt? I lifted my face so it was even with his and kissed him on the lips—a soft kiss that felt so wonderful and familiar. He kissed me back, stronger and deeper this time; I closed my eyes and enjoyed our first kiss in over two months.

Who cares about the germs, I thought, as long as I can kiss Abe.

Wait? Did I just think "Abe"? Omigod, what is going on?

I pulled away from Sam, not even sure if I'd said any of it out loud. He leaned in to kiss me again, so I guess I didn't.

"You know what?" I asked, jumping up and getting out of the swing. "I probably shouldn't have done that."

Sam stood up and put his arms around me. "Just one more?" he asked.

"My parents might—" I gestured toward the house.

"You already have my germs now. What could one more kiss hurt?" He gave me another fabulous, dreamy kiss.

"I love you," he whispered in my ear.

"You have to go," I whispered in his. I took his hand and led him around to the front of the house, and to his car. He leaned against his car and pulled me against him again.

"I can't wait," he said.

"My brothers are watching out the window," I said.

He looked over and sure enough, there were Jeremy and Eli. Eli waved at Sam and Sam gave him a salute, then opened the car door and got in. He banged the door shut and started the car. I went back up on the grass and he pulled away.

By now I was totally confused. My insides were all twisted and my mind was spinning. *How could I want someone this much and still be thinking about someone else? Someone else who hasn't answered my calls or e-mails for three days?*

I walked back into the house, past my brothers, now absorbed in their baseball game again, and up to my room. There I went straight to my computer and looked at Face-book again. He still wasn't there.

Where are you, Abe?

53

It felt like old times when school started, which wasn't such a good thing, but at least I knew this time that it'd be only a month until I could join everyone again. Becca called me every day on the way home from school, and it was a lot more interesting to hear all the news since I'd be back with them all very soon.

I'd started working with my tutor again and kept up with my classes. That was easier, too, knowing the wait would be finite. I never would've expected to be so excited about going back to school!

On the Wednesday after school had started for everyone else, I went back to the hospital for my checkup and biopsy. I saw Dr. Leavens, but Dr. Leavens and Dr. Harrison didn't do biopsies; that was left to the younger doctors. So far most of them had been nice, and it really didn't hurt anymore; they'd become one more thing I had to endure.

This time my doctor was Dr. Gerber, the one I'd met on my prom night ER trip. She was warmer this time and tried to keep some conversation going. I tried to relax as she chattered away.

"Have you had the chance to meet other kids your age that have had transplants?" she asked as she started the biopsy procedure.

"Not too many. Dr. Leavens encouraged me to go to a support group, but I didn't see the need." *Shouldn't she be concentrating more and talking less?*

"I'd think it'd be helpful to talk to other kids," she said.

"It is—I'm friendly with this guy, Abe. I don't know if you know him."

"Yes, I do know Abe. He's in the hospital right now."

I was breathing deeply to avoid feeling the pain of the probe.

"He's getting a biopsy?" *Maybe I can find him and we can have lunch together again and I can finally apologize.*

"No, Emmi. He's been admitted."

"Abe Grant?" I confirmed.

"Yes," she said.

I bolted up. "But why?"

"Emmi, you have to lie down."

I did as I was told.

"What's wrong with Abe?" I asked, getting a little frantic.

"I can't tell you that," she said. "Now, please stay still. We can finish up and you can go see him in the ICU."

"He's in Intensive Care?" I shouted. "What's wrong with him?"

"I still can't tell you that—privacy laws prevent it."

Who cares about privacy laws—my friend was in the ICU and I needed to know why. I lay there for what felt like an eternity; she must have been the slowest biopsy doctor in the history of the world. Then, finally, she was done.

"You need to lie still for a few minutes," Dr. Gerber said, as if this were my first biopsy. I was totally itching to get out of there, but I needed to play along for now. I'd done this enough times to know the doctor typically stepped out of the room when the procedure was over, and sure enough, she did. I counted to fifty, giving her enough time to get down the hall, and then I got dressed, keeping one hand on the bandage on my neck. I stuck my head out the door, and with the coast clear, I bolted. Rushing down the hall to the waiting room I found my mother.

"Mom, Abe's here. He's in the ICU."

I ran out of the waiting room and Mom didn't have a chance to protest; she tossed her coffee cup in the garbage and ran after me. Finding my way to the ICU was no problem; I knew this hospital better than my high school. The elevator was taking too long so we took the stairs, which I ran up two at a time, silently thanking my new heart for letting me do it. By the time Mom opened the door to the ninth floor, we both were panting.

"Stop for a second and catch your breath," Mom said, taking my hand to slow me down.

"I'm fine," I said and kept walking.

Each ICU patient was in their own glass-enclosed room or "pod." I didn't know which one Abe would be in, so I peeked into each one and we didn't need to go far before we spotted Jane sitting outside a room.

"Jane," I shouted and she looked up.

"Emmi, April! What are you doing here?" Jane stood up and walked over to us.

"What's wrong with Abe?" I asked.

"He had pneumonia about a week and a half ago. Not a bad case, but enough to put him in the hospital."

"Is he okay? Why is he in ICU?" I asked. "Shouldn't he be better by now?"

"He should, but unfortunately, he got an infection while he was here."

"From what?" my mother asked.

"They don't know. Could have been anything—even as simple as a nurse not washing his hands, or a stethoscope that was used on someone else and not cleaned."

"That's ridiculous," I protested. "But he's going to be okay, right?"

Jane didn't answer me.

"Jane? What's going on?" I asked, concerned.

"They're having a lot of trouble fighting the infection; they think it's one of those drug-resistant bacteria—it hasn't responded yet to any of the antibiotics they've tried."

"How's his heart?"

"He's not good. Oh, Emmi, they don't know if he's going to make it." And with that Jane started to cry. My mom took her in her arms and gave her a strong hug. "My sisters are in California and can't be here," she said, "so I'm really glad to see you. Thank you, April." Abe's mom shook with sobs and my mom held tight and let her cry.

I had to see Abe. I poked my head into his pod and he was sleeping; then the familiar smell of disinfectant and bad hospital food hit me. I noticed Abe had an IV drip going into his arm—the useless antibiotics. *How can antibiotics not work? Don't they have stronger ones? Are they trying hard enough?*

I stood next to Abe's bed and watched him sleep, his chest moving up and down in rhythm. His face was so sweet; you could tell he was funny and terrific, even asleep. There was something different about him, and then I realized he wasn't wearing his glasses. I leaned over and gave him a tiny kiss on the cheek.

"Abe," I whispered. "Abie," and kissed him again. He moved a little this time, shifting in his sleep. I took his hand and clamped both of mine around it. Then he opened his eyes.

"Emmi?" he asked. "How'd you know I was here?"

"Do you hate me?" I asked him. It had been the question on my mind for the past two weeks.

"God, no," he said. "Why would you ever think that?"

"You were ignoring me—after I got offline so abruptly last week."

"I never noticed—my mom was dragging me out the door to the doctor that day. I'd been sick for a week by then and she was worried." He squeezed my hand and I continued holding his in both of mine.

"Why didn't you tell me?" I asked.

"I didn't want you to worry," he said.

"Didn't you think the not-answering-me thing might worry me more?"

"I haven't been well enough for computer access, and

my mom wouldn't even let me have my cell." Then he took his hand from mine and went to open his robe, wiggling his eyebrows and smirking.

"You can't be that sick if you still want to flash me. What *is it* with that?"

"I don't know. Something about you gives me this overwhelming urge to take off my clothes."

"You're such a perv," I said, laughing.

"Yeah, but I'm a dying perv," he said.

I stopped laughing.

"You're not dying," I said.

"I am, Em. Nothing's working. They're running out of ideas."

I stood there for a second and looked at him. This couldn't be true.

"You can't die."

"Why not?"

"Because if you die, I could die, too. And besides, you can't leave me here all by myself." I was using every bit of control I had not to cry.

"You have Sam," he said.

"I don't want Sam," I said. "I only want you." Until I said it, I didn't even know it was true. But it was.

I looked him in the eye. "I love you, Abe."

That got his attention and he looked at me, disbelieving.

"Sympathy for the dying guy, huh?"

"No, Abe. I've been feeling this way for a while." I kissed him on the cheek and put my face next to his, wrapping my arms around him as much as I could with him lying in a hospital bed.

"Don't mess with me like this, Emmi. I can't deal with it right now."

"I'm not. And you know what? Sometimes skinny and funny is way better than cool and athletic."

"*I'm* cool. Are you saying I'm not cool?"

"You're cool," I giggled. "The question is: are you contagious?"

He smiled. "Not at all." And he leaned over to kiss me. Sam's kisses were nice, but this was Fourth-of-July fireworks awesome.

"I've got to get better now!"

"Yeah, you do."

"I want more of that," he said, and kissed me again. "Only the good die young," he said.

"Don't say that."

"No, 'Only the Good Die Young.' Billy Joel, *The Stranger* album, from 1977. The Catholic Church was totally pissed off at him after that song."

"Tell me more," I said, kissing him again.

"Abe!" Jane said as my mother simultaneously yelled, "Emmi!"

I jumped away from the bed, but looked over at Abe and we both started laughing.

The mothers looked at each other, a little uncomfortable and unsure of how to approach this new situation.

"He's not contagious, Mom," I said. "I asked first."

Abe had on what could only be called a sheepish grin. My mom smiled, but she had a very strained look on her face.

I turned to Abe. "I think we have to go." Abe took my hand and held it. "I'll come back tomorrow. Mom, will you bring me back tomorrow?" I looked at her, pleading. I needed to know when I'd see him again.

"I have to work tomorrow. Why don't we try for Saturday?" she suggested.

I didn't want to wait until Saturday, but I knew I didn't have much choice. It was only three more days; I could wait.

"You get better," I told him. "By the time I see you on Saturday, you're going to be fine." I believed it. I had to—there was no way he couldn't be okay. "Can I call you?" I asked.

"No phones in ICU," Jane said. "I'll try to keep you posted."

My mother took out one of her business cards and wrote our home phone number on the back. "Call us, Jane," Mom said, hugging her. "Even if you just need a friendly ear. I'm happy to listen."

"We're going to be okay," Jane said.

I wanted—no, I *needed*—to believe her.

54

"Why hasn't Jane called?" I asked my mother as we ate dinner Friday night. The boys were both at their sports practices, so it was a quiet meal for me and my parents. "It's been two days—that can't be good." I moved the lentils and rice around my plate; I hadn't eaten much since we'd been to the hospital and I couldn't think about much else besides Abe.

"Call the hospital," I demanded.

"And say what?" my mother asked.

"Call to see if he's still—you know—that he didn't . . . That he's okay." I couldn't say the dreaded D-word.

"Dan, do you know anyone over at the hospital you could call?"

"Why don't you ask Dr. Leavens?" my dad suggested.

"Yeah, call Dr. Leavens," I said, hopping up to give my mother the phone.

"She's not going to be in now—it's dinnertime. Get in the car, Emmi. Let's just go to the hospital." I ran upstairs, grabbed my iPod, and started back down, but then I sat on the steps to listen to my parents arguing in the kitchen.

"Aren't visiting hours over?" my father asked.

"We know everyone over there—they'll let us up," my mother answered. She grabbed her shoulder bag, looked around the counter for her car keys, found them, and walked into the hallway. I crept back to the top of the stairs so they couldn't see me.

"Why are you encouraging her with this? What if he dies? Or he's already dead?"

"Stop it. This boy means a lot to her; I can't just let her sit here and worry."

"You're setting her up for a huge letdown."

My mom put her arms around my father. "Dan, she needs to know. Now, not in the morning. Don't you remember being that age and totally irrational?"

"I was never irrational."

"What about the time we tried to break into your basement window to fool around and you smashed the window and took a chunk out of your arm?" She smiled at him. My dad looked down at his arm. I always wondered where he'd gotten that scar.

"Okay, you win. But take care of her—please."

She kissed him and turned to call me, and our eyes met. I mouthed a "thank you."

We got to the hospital quickly, since rush hour was over; then, going through the doors, we greeted the security guard as usual.

"Hi, Emmi. Good evening, Mrs. Miller," the security guard said as we passed. Mom was right; they didn't question why we were coming in.

273

We took the elevator to the ninth floor and went down the hall to find Abe; I didn't know what was going to happen when we got there, but I knew I had to see him.

We got to his pod and looked through the glass to see Jane sitting in a chair next to Abe, who slept. She had a magazine on her lap, but she was staring off into space. When Mom and I stepped into the room, we startled Jane; one look at her red eyes told us the news wasn't good. She explained that Abe was on a ventilator now; he was too sick to breathe on his own.

"The infection's everywhere now," Jane whispered. "His kidneys have shut down and so has his liver."

"How's his heart?" my mother asked.

"Bad," Jane said. "And they can't consider retransplanting him with the infection. "

"How are you?" Mom asked. Jane shrugged, then began to cry. My mother put her arms around Jane, then walked her out into the hallway.

I walked over and looked at Abe; he looked a little distorted with the breathing tube, but I kissed him on the cheek and whispered in his ear. I didn't know if he could hear me, but I had things I needed to say to him.

"Abe. It's me, Emmi. I'm here, and I love you." I took a breath and looked at him.

"It's not looking like you're going to be okay, Abe, and I can't believe it. I don't think I can go on without you, but I know if you heard me say that, you'd yell at me and probably make a joke, then tell me it was nonsense.

"But Abe, if you're not around, who's going to flash

me and tell me about classic rock music, and make me laugh when I've had it with pills and biopsies and the moon face and everything?" The tears were flowing now. "I don't know if I can do it without you, Abe." I stifled a sob.

"But I know what you need," I said, and then went to my bag, pulling out my iPod. I put one earphone in his ear and one in mine. I went to my "Abe's Playlist" and found "Freebird" by Lynyrd Skynyrd. Then I put my head on his chest, closed my eyes, and breathed in and out, matching his breaths as the music played.

"If I leave here tomorrow? Would you still remember me?" I sang along with the band.

Abe said this song was his father's favorite part of the concerts he worked on, and thinking about this gave me another idea and I sat up.

"Abe," I said. "Soon you're going to be with your father. Did I ever tell you that I believe that when you die, you see all the people you loved and who've died before you? That's so great, Abe." I felt a strange comfort in it— that the boy who spent his whole life trying to hold on to his father was finally going to be with him now.

My mom and Jane came back in the room.

"Let us stay with you tonight," my mom offered.

"I don't know," Jane replied, hesitating.

I went to the two women and pleaded, "Please, Jane."

"Thank you both so much. But I think I'd like to be alone with him tonight. I'm sorry."

"I understand," Mom said. "We'll come back in the morning." I really wanted to stay; I needed to be there, in that room with Abe, but I respected Jane's wishes.

"Bye, Abe," I whispered, kissing his forehead. "I'll see you tomorrow." *Please still be with us tomorrow. Please fight, Abe.*

Mom and I had started walking down the hall when Jane came chasing after us.

"Emmi, you forgot your iPod," she said, holding it out to me.

"Let Abe listen to it tonight," I said.

She hesitated, looking down at the iPod; then, with a pained smile, she said, "I think he'd like that." She turned and walked back to her dying only child's room.

Mom and I drove home in silence; there just wasn't anything left to say. When we pulled in to our driveway and got out of the car, I said "Thank you, Mom," She put her arm around me and we walked into the house together.

I didn't sleep much that night; at three a.m. I gave up and turned on the light, then went over to the computer. I almost expected to see Abe's name on the chat list. Then, glancing at the collages of photos on my wall, I realized I didn't have a single picture of him. *How am I going to remember him if I don't have a picture?* I went through all of my memories of our times together, thinking about him and burning every one of the images into my brain; I wanted to be sure it'd all be imprinted there forever.

My eyes had just started to close when the phone rang in my parents' room. I slipped into the hallway and heard my mother answer it.

"Oh, Jane," she wailed, and I knew.

55

I'm not sure how I got through the next few days—it was all a blur. I have vague memories of Mom bringing my meds and encouraging me to drink protein shakes. I couldn't eat, but I managed a few sips of the shakes. Even in my sorrow, I knew I had to eat something—I couldn't let myself fall apart.

My mother called Becca, who came over and sat with me for a while; holding my hand, she listened to all my Abe stories. I knew that if I could still talk about him, it'd be like he was still alive.

I didn't know what anyone told Sam; I had to face him at some point, but I had no idea what I was going to say.

My family didn't leave me alone for a minute: some-one—one of my brothers, or one of my parents—or Becca—was always by my side.

On the morning of the funeral, I stood there for a long time staring into my closet, unable to focus enough to find the right outfit. *What do you wear to say goodbye to some-one you love this much?*

Then, almost as if she knew, my mother came in, and, finding me motionless in front of the closet, she guided me out of the way. She went in and pulled out my best black slacks and a pink blouse. She brought out my black belt and black dress shoes and even found a pair of socks for me, laying them all on the bed next to where I sat.

"Do you need help getting dressed?"

I looked down at the clothes on the bed and shook my head. "No, thanks. I can handle it," I said, staring at the clothes.

My brain struggled to process the idea of taking off my pajamas and putting on the dress clothes. It was such a simple thing, but I wasn't sure I could manage.

"Emmi, someone's here to see you," Eli shouted from downstairs.

"Who?"

"It's Sam." I looked out my window and sure enough, his car was outside. *Why is he here? What can I say to him?*

I managed to get dressed and go downstairs; Sam was sitting in the family room talking to Eli. He was wearing a suit and tie.

"See you later, Sam," Eli said, leaving the room. Sam stood up and walked over to me.

"I'm so sorry, Emmi," he said.

"Thanks." I couldn't meet his eyes.

"I know how much he meant to you." *No you don't— you have no idea.* "And I'm so sorry I gave you a hard time about him." I didn't answer him—I couldn't. "Can I come with you today? I want to be there for you."

I shook my head no. "I need to do this alone, Sam. Abe and I—we—well, we were . . ." I glanced up at him; he looked so hurt.

"I thought so." He said it so quietly, I could barely hear him.

"You look handsome, though." He did, but I didn't love him. Not like I loved Abe. "You're going to be the best-dressed guy at school today, right?" He smiled at me.

Several weeks ago that smile would have melted me, but now—nothing. Sam walked out and got into his car, but I didn't watch him go.

My parents and my brothers went with me; it was a weekday, so it was nice of them to take the time off from work, school, and sports to do this for me. And, as much as I'd always complained about my brothers, what we all went through in the past year made me realize what great kids they were.

I guess some people would say Abe's funeral was beautiful. But where's the beauty in a funeral for a sixteen-year-old boy? Abe told his mother he wanted an outdoor graveside service, and that's exactly what she'd arranged.

People were milling around when we arrived. I saw Leo and Morty and gave them a little wave.

Jane was standing by the grave with two women who looked like an older and younger variation of her. I noticed that her hair was completely gray now, as if it'd transformed overnight. She looked so much older now than when I first met her at the hospital, when we all had lunch together.

"Emmi," she said when she saw me walking toward

her. "Come meet my sisters." I went with her and she introduced me to Abe's aunts. "Emmi was a very good friend to Abe—probably the best friend he ever had."

I smiled uncomfortably. "He was good to me, too." Jane hugged me and we held on to each other for a minute.

"I brought your iPod," she said. "We're going to play some of the music during the funeral; you know how Abe was about his music."

I nodded, thinking about how passionate he was about those old rock bands.

Then I noticed an older man who was making his way toward her. He was dressed in a tailored gray suit and a red tie; his hair was brown with gray at the temples that matched his suit.

Jane gasped.

"Who is that?" I asked Abe's aunt. All three women were silent. "Do you know him?" I asked.

It was Jane who finally spoke: "That's Abe's father," she said. "And I can't believe he's here."

Can't believe he's here? I can't believe he's alive.

"But Abe told me his father was dead," I said.

"He found it easier to say that, rather than explain that he left us for another woman and had another family with her."

"But Abe said he was an engineer for some rock bands, and that he went back on the road. And died in a bus crash!"

Jane chuckled. "He's an engineer, for a small air-conditioning company in Canton, Ohio."

What? "Then why did Abe . . ." This was way too confusing.

"Isn't it a better story Abe's way?" Jane asked. "His father was a roadie one summer for Lynyrd Skynyrd when he was eighteen, but the rest Abe made up."

I looked over at this man who'd left his little boy; and I thought about the boy who'd loved him so much, he'd made up a whole different life around him.

"Then where'd he get all those concert T-shirts?" I asked, baffled by what I was hearing.

"eBay," Jane said with a little laugh. "Abe hasn't seen him in over ten years; he wasn't around for any of it. Not the hospitalizations, not the transplant. And *now* he shows up?" She walked away from us, toward the man in the gray suit—to Abe's father—who was alive and living in Ohio.

"Think she'll let him stay?" one sister asked the other.

"Yes, I do. I think she'll realize Abe would have wanted him here."

"No, Abe actually wanted him here when he was alive. This is crazy," I said and stormed over to confront Abe's father.

How could you do this to Abe? Where were you when he needed you? Your son loved you so much! He even made up elaborate stories about you and became a rock historian to cling to something about you. And you just sat there in Ohio with your other family and ignored him—even when he was dying. And now you show up? When he can't even appreciate your being here?

I was ready to scream all of these things at Abe's dad, but Jane was crying in his arms and he was sobbing, too. I walked away shaking my head, allowing them their private moment.

The funeral service commenced, and Abe's mom and dad stood together as they lowered the casket into the ground.

I couldn't believe Abe's skinny body was in that box; I couldn't believe he wasn't going to come and flash me, or tell me more rock 'n roll facts: things like Eric Clapton's nickname was Slow Hand, and the Beatles' first drummer was Pete Best.

How could he not be around to tell me what else to expect with the transplant aftereffects, or how long until the moon face goes away? I'd learned so much from him.

I was going to miss him so much.

Someone turned on my iPod, which was plugged into portable speakers, and a familiar song came on. It was "Don't Stop" by Fleetwood Mac. They were actually playing Fleetwood Mac at Abe's funeral. After Lynyrd Skynyrd, they were probably his favorite band. I smiled, remembering the background on the band he gave me about members dating, then breaking up, and how they used it all when they wrote the songs for *Rumours*. He so totally loved this band.

The grown-ups around the gravesite smiled in recognition, and they even started tapping their feet to the beat. It was all kind of unconventional, but it was so Abe-like.

Jane leaned over to me and said, "He wanted me to play this song for you, Emmi."

So I listened to the lyrics about moving on even when you didn't think you could, and always looking ahead, toward tomorrow.

He was letting me go and telling me to live my life.

That was my amazing guy—still thinking about how to help me—even at the very end.

Oh, Abe.

56

October first finally came—the day I'd been waiting for for so long. I was going back to school and playing soccer—in other words, my old life. Not that I'd ever be who I was again.

This time last year, my biggest worries were how my hair looked and if we'd win a soccer game. Now I had a twice-daily reminder—whenever I took my meds—of how close I'd come to dying. I'd learned that for me to stay alive, someone else had to die; and I now knew that sometimes people die, and that life doesn't have to be fair.

Even though I was looking forward to seeing my friends, I wasn't sure how much patience I'd have for all the usual nonsense: who likes whom, who isn't talking to whom, who's wearing the wrong outfit, and who's gained a little weight—in other words, the typical day-to-day stupid worries of the average high school senior.

For a while after Abe died, I was angry that so much was taken from me. But then it occurred to me that sometimes things happen for a reason, even though I couldn't come up with one that explained why I had to go through all this. Who knows? Maybe it was to gain perspective—to see that you don't have to run away every time you face adversity. Or maybe it was so Abe could have the chance to touch my life.

Not everything had changed—I still had some of the same goals: I hadn't given up my dream of playing soccer in college; it wasn't going to be easy, but after what I'd been through this year, I figured I could make it happen. My college essay would be more interesting than most; it wouldn't be the usual stuff about what I did on my summer vacations.

When you're sixteen, you think you're invincible; you feel like you're immortal and that nothing can ever touch you—and this year I learned it's not true.

This year I learned that my parents looked out for me, and that my brothers would always be there for me. And that skinny and funny were sometimes better than cool and athletic—it just depended on who had those traits.

I got through my first day back at school without too much incident, but I knew there was some pointing and whispering behind my back. My friends welcomed me back with open arms—literally. There were so many of them hugging me, I ended up late for first period. Some geeky sophomore from the school newspaper wanted to interview me about my transplant; I told him I'd have to think about it; I wasn't sure I was ready for publicity yet. But it might be better than everyone wondering, and making up things that weren't true. (I'd already heard two girls whispering that I'd been in a coma for six weeks.)

I even had a class with Sam—honors English. I'd snuck a glance at him a few times, and once he was looking at me, too; we shared a sweet smile. I'm not sure we can ever go back, but who knows. I guess we'll always have a connection.

The school day is over and I'm in the locker room to change. I'm totally psyched for soccer practice and have a lot of catching up to do—a month is already gone from this season.

Lacing my cleats for the first time in ten months feels great—and familiar. The team hits the field and starts doing stretches, all of us forming a circle. I look around at these girls I've played soccer with my whole life and smile, thinking of everything we've shared and everything that's ahead of us. It's amazing to be back here, where I belong.

The sun's out, the field freshly mowed (I so love that smell), and life's good. I'm here to run around.

I'm here. *It's a good place to be.*

Author's Note

Nearly 106,000 people in the United States are desperate to receive organ transplants—not just hearts, but also livers, lungs, kidneys and other organs. Each day, approximately 18 people die in the U.S. because of the acute shortage of organ donors. And, every 11 minutes a new name is added to the waiting list. It's tragic and frustrating to think about how many donor organs are lost simply because individuals didn't sign up to be donors, or else their families said no when they were asked.

It's not easy to think about your own death or that of a loved one. But if the worst were to happen, an organ donor may save as many as eight lives—just by the simple act of registering to be an organ donor.

Now that you've read *Change of Heart*, I hope you will enroll in the organ donor registry in your state (you must be 18 to register), and that you will ask your relatives and friends to sign up.

For more information , please visit **Donate Life America** at www.donatelife.net.

Acknowledgments

I have to start where it all began: my parents, Lorraine and Stan Berger. They have supported me in every way and I would not be at this point without their incredible presence.

Marlene Stringer, my fabulous agent, has been a guiding force and a wonderful resource for the whirlwind journey to publication.

Evelyn Fazio, editor/publisher extraordinaire, thank you for believing in *Change of Heart*. Thanks to everyone at WestSide for their ongoing diligence.

Huge kudos to my critique group: Dawn Buthorn and Jill Arabas. My writing and spirit are always stronger after our sessions. Arlene Sandner, of the New City Library, was an early fan of Emmi and I'm so appreciative of the time she takes to read my books. I'm grateful to everyone who read and commented through all of the early drafts, including my teen readers.

This book could never have been written without guidance on the medical side. I was lucky enough to speak to several posttransplant patients. They are all amazingly strong people who generously shared their experiences with me, making Emmi's journey real. Special thanks to Dr. Linda Addonizio and my own personal reference physician, Dr. Mathew Maurer (more on him later).

My New City friends help me juggle kids and keep me sane. Big thanks to all the Bergers and Maurers for everything (especially much-needed vacations!).

At the core of it all is my family. Lissie, Josh, and Eric, thanks for letting me steal tiny bits of your lives to give to Emmi and her brothers. And, this never could have happened without my husband, Mat. Besides his endless patience with my never-ending cardiac "what ifs," he has been by my side whispering words of encouragement since we were seventeen years old. What a great ride we've had together.